Augusta Joyce Crocheron

The Children's Book

A collection of short stories and poems. A Mormon book for Mormon children.

Augusta Joyce Crocheron

The Children's Book
A collection of short stories and poems. A Mormon book for Mormon children.

ISBN/EAN: 9783337297671

Printed in Europe, USA, Canada, Australia, Japan

Cover: Foto ©Andreas Hilbeck / pixelio.de

More available books at **www.hansebooks.com**

THE

CHILDREN'S BOOK.

A Collection of Short Stories and Poems;

A MORMON BOOK FOR MORMON CHILDREN.

By AUGUSTA JOYCE CROCHERON.

BOUNTIFUL, DAVIS CO., UTAH:
PUBLISHED FOR THE AUTHOR.
1890.

PREFACE.

A Little Talk with the Children.

The thought came into my mind, *Write a book for the children;* and while I listened, it became a desire and a pleasant one, for I would dearly love to become the household friend of many little children who are growing up within the homes of the Saints.

If they are willing to listen, I will tell them a few true stories, not fairy ones, indeed, of which little ones are so fond, so fascinating, but, alas! so false. No, these must be true.

Many pleasant hours have I spent in story-telling, and surely my pleasure was as great as theirs ; stories to sleepy eyes, out in the summer moonlight on the veranda, with great patches of flowers faintly showing in the shadows of wide branches, and night-birds singing over us; story-telling on rainy afternoons, or by roaring hearth-light ; at home and abroad—how many listeners there have been. But I must not tell you what I have read, as I did those little hearers, it must be some things that I have known. If I could only show to my little friends of the present time, the sweet faces remembered looking anxiously into mine, it would be the best part of the book ; those—no story could equal.

Would that I could make these, also, my friends, as the authors I so loved were mine.

(iii)

And, if I should ever travel from home, as some of the Sisters do, to visit the associations, I would be happy to have you tell me, if we meet, if anything written herein has pleased you.

Pleasant smiles and kind words from good hearts are sometimes worth more than silver and gold.

This book is the fulfillment of a wish expressed by President Brigham Young a short time before his death, and in conclusion he said, "Who will write a book for the children?"

To attempt this was in my power, but it required means to publish, and this I could not do alone. Two good Brethren, who think more of the youth of our people than they do of riches, were kind enough to lend me the use of what was needed to accomplish the object.

When you read this book, I want you in your hearts to thank Bishop Jacob Weiler, of Third Ward, Salt Lake City, and Elder Alwood Brown, of Centreville, Davis County, and ask our Heavenly Father to bless and prosper them long upon the earth, and may their names be held by you in pure and lasting remembrance.   AUGUSTA JOYCE CROCHERON.

Bountiful, Davis County, Utah,
   September 3, 1890.

This
Book is Dedicated
To the Sweetest and Best of
all Children, and Every
Mother has It.

CONTENTS.

(vii)

CONTENTS.

List of Illustrations.

(x)

THE
Children's Book.

Energy of Character.

MANY young persons are apt to feel as though the future held nothing special in store for them, to inspire their present energies of thought and labor, and so pass idly and indifferently through precious years of time.

Some are checked by obstacles seemingly insurmountable, but if I may relate to such a true story, perhaps a few might gather encouragement therefrom and start with fresh ardor in the pursuit of some fondly-cherished object in life, for surely no one among our young people in this favored country can be found in so discouraging a condition of circumstances as was my hero, Joseph H. Whitmore.

Somewhere in Novia Scotia (I have forgotten the name of the place) was a vast field of coal mines where many men, women, and children were employed.

A person of good education and considerable ex-

(11)

perience, having traveled much abroad, became at one time superintendent of a large force of these miners.

He had met and heard the Mormon elders and opposed them, not only in public gatherings, but also by printed letters and pamphlets. When he later became superintendent of this large mine, although abundantly able to keep his children at school, he preferred to rear them in ignorance and servitude, and one by one they left him and emigrated to Long Island to earn their own living away from him. Joseph was one of his youngest children, but when he was only six years of age his father one morning announced that he, too, must go to work in the coal mines. Little readers, look at your little brothers or playmates of that age and try to imagine a Utah-born child condemned to such a life. Would not our enemies make a great commotion over such cruelty?

Early one morning, before daylight, he was aroused from his sweet sleep to dress, eat, and go to work.

I cannot help thinking that he must have rubbed his blue eyes very hard to keep them open, that he did not eat much breakfast at that hour, that he went out into the darkness with timid step, and that his loving mother must have been very sad at heart, and missed all day long his cheerful voice, happy face, and quick footsteps.

Entering the mine beside his father, he was shown his work, which was to load up a little box on wheels with small, loose lumps of coal in corners too low for larger persons to enter. Another little boy drew the box by a short chain fastened to a leather belt around his waist, as he crept along on his hands and knees, like a little animal, for the way was too low for him to stand upright until he reached one of the larger passages, where he emptied his load upon a large pile, where, in turn, men and women loaded wheelbarrows and took the coal farther along.

In one of these places stood a large pail or keg of beer, with a dipper in it, and both sexes, old and young, helped themselves. Little Joseph was sadly frightened at his dark and wicked surroundings, but dared not complain. He thought how much rather he would prefer to work for his gentle mother all day long and never murmur, but such could not be his lot. At nine years he was considered old enough and large enough to draw a little wagon instead of loading one. At twelve years he was set to shoveling coal, and one day a large amount became loosened from the side wall and fell upon him in such a shape as to cover him like a large lid, without breaking any of his limbs, although several of his finger nails were completely scraped away. Through the huge mass he could hear men striking with picks and swearing, while his father seemed greatly excited, fearing to find only the mangled remains of his son. Joseph was taken out and carried home to a bed of long and severe sickness, but for which he felt thankful, for in all the precious six years he had never seen the outside world by the light of day; he had gone to his work before daylight and returned after dark, Sundays included.

At the expiration of two months he was obliged to
go back.   Had it not been for his Christian mother,
whose whispers to her poor boy gently sustained him,
his heart would have grown hard and wicked; but
she had often told him a time for his release would
come if he would be patient; that the good Lord
would in time answer her daily prayers for him.

When in his fourteenth year, another cave occurred
in the mine, and this time his hands were severely
bruised, his bare feet also.   Every nail upon feet and
hands came off; but the severest injury rested on his
eyes, which were so filled with fine coal that it was
feared he would be forever blind.   Many weeks passed,
during which only one voice whispered hope to him—
his mother's.   During this period of suffering and
suspense, his father declared he would not send him
back into the mine if he ever got well.   When Joseph
was able to walk around, his anxious mother asked
him if he did not think it would be wisdom for him to
go to his married sister in Long Island, for she feared
his father would revoke his promise and send him
again to the mine, and she had little confidence that
he would again be so fortunate as to escape with his
life if similar accidents should again occur.

Joseph dreaded to part from that dear mother who
had been his only comfort all these years; he thought
of the children she had buried, and that one only beside him remained at home; but she bade him go into
the free, wide world until he became a man, then she
would look for him to come home to her once more.

Long they talked and wept together, and that night
the mother gathered together his scanty clothing. In
the morning she asked his father's permission for
Joseph to go to his sister and learn her husband's trade
—stone-cutting. The father readily agreed and gave
him money "to get off as soon as possible." That
day Joseph turned with breaking heart from mother
and sister and took passage for Long Island, where he
found a welcome and began in the new trade. A year
later his young sister followed him, and found employment with a dressmaker.

One afternoon Joseph, now eighteen years old, in
company with a companion apprentice, was returning
from some work, when they noticed an unusual throng
going into an institution of learning. By attention
they learned that it was a grand examination-day and
that visitors were going in. After a brief consultation,
in which curiosity was uppermost, they slipped in
with the rest and watched proceedings with great interest. At the conclusion of the exercises, they men-
tally expressed themselves that they did not know
before that anyone could learn so much, and each pro-
posed to go to school. They lingered around outside
waiting for the principal, at sight of whom Joseph's
companion lost courage and hurried off. Joseph,
however, was so fascinated that he followed the professor home to his door before daring to speak, when
he was discovered by that gentleman, who kindly inquired his errand. Pitying the youth's confusion, he
invited him in, soon won his confidence, and asked

him a number of questions. Poor Joseph did not
know how to write a line, although eighteen years
old, leaving the matter of correspondence entirely to
his brother-in-law; but the kind old professor talked
with him and invited himself to visit Joseph next day.
He was so pleased with what he learned that he gave
him private lessons during the month's vacation, and
when the new term began, Joseph entered the primary
department, from which he very soon graduated. For
Joseph a new life had opened, and a year passed rapidly away.

One evening his young sister regarded him so pen-
sively he asked her what she was thinking of. " Joe,
dear, you are getting ahead of me," and she broke
down and cried. It did not take him more than a
minute to decide that they should go to school six
months each, alternately. Not wishing to impose on
their kind relatives, they agreed to hire two small
rooms and to keep house, he to work at his trade for
their support while she attended school, and then she
to sew in an establishment while he resumed his
studies. This devoted brother and sister passed two
happy years in this manner, each enlivening and as-
sisting the other in their cozy evenings. At last this
beautiful arrangement was broken up by one of the
teachers in the academy wishing the good and gentle
girl to adorn his own comfortable and elegant home.

When Joseph was twenty-one years of age, he returned to visit his dear old mother for a few months;
but she told him her labors were finished, her soul was

satisfied, and she was soon going to her little ones, where sorrow could never reach her spirit any more. A few weeks longer beside her, days of tenderest peace and love, nights of gentlest, patient watching, listening for feeble whispers, lifting the weary head to rest upon his bosom, as she had once done for him, and then at last to bow in lowliness and prayer as she, too, had done beside her precious babes. His own hand chiseled the pure white tablet that bore the record of her sainted life, and when he left his childhood's home, there was nothing in face, or voice, or scene, to call him back again.

Joseph returned to Long Island and became imbued with the spirit of a missionary, to teach the ignorant and indifferent. The ragged, the truant, the street idlers, he would talk with and lure within the school-room walls, and interest them so that they would soon desire to come. If one were absent, that night he would visit and inquire if sickness, or what cause, had prevented attendance, and always with a bunch of flowers, an orange, or some pretty card for the absentee. Saturdays, in fine weather, there was often a short stroll, when a brief lesson in botany, sketching, or some other study, was brought up in connection with the surroundings. He became to them more than a teacher—a dear friend. Many lessons not in their books were learned, and by example he taught refinement, religion, nobility, and love When one of his little pupils died, it was the teacher who carved the white monument that marks the rest-

2

ing-place of Frankie; a scroll enwreathed with rose-
buds, a lasting monument of the love between master
and pupil; those days of patient labor, the token of a
pure bond between soul and soul.

This teacher became my instructor also, and later I
was his assistant. For a year he boarded with my
parents, and it was from his own life the facts of this
little story were gathered. While he was with us he
received a large album filled with the photographs of
one hundred former pupils, children he had gathered
in from the alleys and haunts of idleness and evil,
but now reclaimed, industrious, and honorable.

We could not but join in his happiness, so sincere
and genuine that tears mingled with his laughter as
he read the accompanying letter and compared the
autographs and portraits. "Shoe Black Jim," "Limpy
Dick," "Match-box Maggie," and many others—how
glad he was to see them! "I'm an office-boy now,"
"I'm a telegraph messenger," "I'm going to be a stone-
cutter, where you began"—such were the little mes-
sages that came to him.

When we left home for Utah, this gentleman traveled with us one day's journey and turned back in the
morning. We were of one faith and he of another,.
but, with true courtesy, he never became unpleasant
in his discussions upon Mormonism, during all our
acquaintance. He wished my parents "Godspeed,
and every good in this life and hereafter."

Often I compared in my own mind his boyhood, so
bleak and devoid of promise, then his manhood, so

useful and exemplary, with so great a prospect before him, and thought, None need despair, God can deliver and lift up from the depths, into light and into his service. Children of the saints, strive to write your names upon the hearts of the tried, the sorrowful, and tempted.

— — · —

A Story of Faith.

SOME years ago a lady removed from Utah to California to join her father, for she was a widow with little children, and in the struggle to provide for them by her own labor, her health was gone, and she gladly turned to the parent who offered to help her.

After a few months, feeling her strength somewhat restored, she decided to take some mechanics as boarders, as she could thus relieve her father of his kind obligation, and yet be within his protection.

Sometimes at the end of the week there was not much money left to go on with, but her credit at the store next door was good, and so she kept on, hoping for better times, while still thankful to be able to eat the food of her own earning.

The winter had been unusually rainy, the streets were shining with little currents of muddy water, and the children were kept in-doors. One Monday morning her little boy, awaking from his sleep at her side, asked: "Mamma, when will I have a pair of boots? I have wanted them so long." The mother's heart ached, for she knew that the poor things she tied on his feet every morning were no protection, though they had once been good shoes—though of course even the best of shoes do not last forever. But she answered, consolingly: "You must be very good and prayerful to get those boots, darling. I have only enough money to start the week with, but I hope to get them for you soon." "Yes, mamma," he answered, as she kissed him, and then rose from her bed to go and cook breakfast for the men.

After she passed into the hall, a little noise arrested her steps. Was he covering his head to cry with disappointment? As she softly turned back to the door ajar, she saw that he had slipped out of bed and was kneeling beside a chair, and prayed: "O Lord, my heavenly Father, I do want a pair of boots; I have wanted them so long, red-top boots, and my mother has so little money; won't you please send me a pair? Amen." The little boy opened his eyes in faith, looked up to the ceiling, all around his chair, first on his knees and then standing, and a shade of disappointment crossed his face. In another moment he had decided. "He knelt down again and shut those blessed eyes and said his prayer over once more," said his mother, and she turned away with a heart full of painful emotions and went silently to her kitchen. Just as breakfast was ready, one of the boarders entered the room and went directly to her.

'Mrs. Cole, if you will accept of them, here is a pair of boots, a New Year's present for your little boy." She thanked him and opened the paper, and her heart leaped to see a pair of red-topped boots! "Come here, pet," she called, and the little fellow obeyed quickly, giving a cry of delight as he saw the gift. Trembling with joy, he hastened to pull them on, but —they were too small! Choking with grief and disappointment, he cried, brokenly : " O Lord, when you knew the size of my feet, why did you send the boots too small ? " Almost as he spoke, another of the boarders came in, and, not seeming to notice the group around the boy, addressed the mother as the first one had done. Thanking him also, she tore off the wrapper, and there was another pair of red-topped boots a size larger, and in one leg a pair of light red woolen stockings. As the little fellow fairly got into them, he lifted up his happy face, all smiles and tears, saying: " Oh, He remembered those were too small and sent these right after! "

The men looked inquiringly and in amazement, but the mother replied by a significant look, and they waited for her explanation by and by. Said the giver of the first pair, "I'll take these back and get you a lovely hat," and darted out. In a few moments he returned with the hat, and the difference in value in small change, which he handed the happy boy.

Four days after this a near neighbor (their houses almost joined) came in dejectedly, and said : " I don't know what to do, I'm out of flour, and—" "Why

don't you ask the Lord for flour? He'll send it to
you," said our little hero.

The woman was surprised, and answered confusedly,
"Yes, but—" "Don't you ever ask the Lord for
things when you want them? If you don't, it's time
for you to begin." And seeing her bewildered look
increasing, he asked, sweetly and gently: "Don't you
know what to say? Come with me, I'll tell you,"
and he caught her hand with such pleading earnestness that the woman followed him into an inner room,
and, kneeling down before a chair, she followed his
example, and he said, sweetly, "Say it with me."
As the woman began to repeat after him, these
thoughts rushed through the mother's mind: If his
prayer is not fulfilled, my child's faith will be shaken.
She slipped into the store next door, and, saying
quickly, "I'll pay for this," picked up a small sack of
flour and hurried away with it.

The visitor went home in a reflective mood, but
hastily returned, exclaiming: "Mrs. Cole, when I
reached home there was a sack of flour on my door-
step." Said the darling boy, "I knew God would
hear you."

The mother, afterwards, explained it all to her friend,
but never to her boy; to God she gave the glory.

"And is your son still a praying boy?" I asked
her when she told me the beautiful story of years
gone by. "Yes, he is still a prayerful boy, and said
to me when I came away here on a visit, 'Mother,
don't be anxious or lonely; I shall pray for you every
day.'"

So the seed of faith sown in the heart of a Latter-day Saint child, born here in Utah, lived, bloomed, and bore its fruit afar in another land.

Little readers, this story is as true a one as could be told.

A Fable.

Showing the Descent of Ignoble Pride and the Elevation of Humble Merit.

SAID a clean plate to a dish-cloth, as it leaned back with an indolent air of superiority against the cupboard wall: "Dear me, how you look! Move away from me, I request you."

"Ah me!" sighed the dish-cloth, "I once was a piece of cloth, unbroken, and as white as you. It is the keeping you tidy that has brought me to this complexion. I can remember when, after clearing away the distresses that clouded your face, how you have beamed brightly upon me. Think of the many times I have gone through hot and cold water for you. What would you soon look like without me?"

"Oh," replied the plate, "dish-cloths are plenty enough, there's no trouble about that; besides, what have you done more than your duty? Were it not for plates, what need would there be of dish-cloths? You owe your very existence to the fact of our having a

use for you. Be content to fill your proper sphere
without repining, and consider it sufficient honor.
Your labors are not arduous; we plates bear the burdens and represent your class for you; our very appearance is an acknowledgment that dish-cloths are an
auxiliary of our private life. Be assured you are
where you belong; what else could you have been,
anyway?"

Said the meek dish-cloth: "I find that I have several
answers to make to what you have just spoken. In
simply doing my duty I have been plunged into nau-
seous floods of dish-water, twisted and wrung in every
fiber of my frame, and then shaken almost to pieces before I wiped your face, and, after all my tortures and
labors, have hung patiently and conveniently near
you on a nail ready at an instant's notice to attend
you again. As to owing my existence to the fact of
there being china in the world, that is scarcely posi-
tive. I was descended from the notable family of Flax,
and took the preparatory degrees of my class with
care and exactitude. I might have become a sheet or
a pillow-case. Some of my cousins are fine towels and
wear the finest borders and fringes, and wait upon the
faces of persons instead of plates. Still others of the
Flax family are fine table-napery, and continually mingle among the most distinguished company. A distant branch of our family belongs to the high order of
handkerchiefs and laces, and the elegance of their appearance and belongings is seldom surpassed. Although I seldom appear out of this sphere of action,

my ideas are not confined to it, and on wash-days, thanks to the laundress, the fresh air and sunshine refresh me and help me to bear my retired life with, I think, sufficient composure. But for your lofty manner and unkind salutation just now, I would have made no reference to the unpleasant conditions of a monotonous life."

Just here a honeysuckle and a climbing rose on opposite sides of the open window nodded their heads at each other and threw a breath of their sweetest perfume into the patient dish-cloth, and looked their very brightest and sweetest toward it. A humming-bird darted angrily back and forth, and seemed to be trying to drown the buzzing questions of a pompous bumble-bee with his own noise, and a morning-glory vine rung her bells as if calling them to order. A wandering, pirouetting flirt of a whirlwind waltzed by just then, fairly near enough to stir the skirts of the dish-cloth, but the noise startled the dozing cat, who, exclaiming, " Mouse ! " jumped from the cook's chair. This sudden movement jarred the cupboard a little, and, to its dismay, the plate, still in a lounging attitude, lost its equilibrium, and, staggering vainly, was next moment seen flat on its back, with the noonday sun glaring hotly in its face.

"Assist me," it called to the humble partner of its late conversation. Whether the nail clung tenaciously to the dish-cloth, or whether the latter was too exhausted by labor and the sadness of a wounded spirit, was not made known to this narrator, but, although it seemed to sway gently to and fro as though trying to hitch off and down, the effort was useless. At last the dish-cloth replied: " My friend, it is impossible for me to help you in this calamity; your case requires aid from an abler source. Were I near you, I could only shield you from the sun but could not lift you. Wait, I beg of you, with resignation until the cook appears." A contemptuous silence followed. It seemed to the plate just then that the clock glared down upon it and said deliberately: " See there! see there! ha! ha! ha! ha!" and that the tea-kettle was whistling a most unsympathetic air, and the lid dancing a disrespectful jig, as much as to say, "I keep myself on my feet; I'm a water drinker."

It had been rumored in the kitchen after a dinner-party some time previously that this same fine plate had come from the dining-room smelling of brandy or something, and the plate's present prone condition apparently revived the unpleasant suggestion.

However, before this went any further, and an exoneration or proof of the insinuation was given, and thereby all unpleasant feelings between these parties done away with, the cook suddenly entered, accompanied by her mistress, with book in hand, to superintend the making of a fine pudding. Their remarks soon conveyed the information that a large number of guests were coming to dinner that afternoon.

A happy and triumphant thought occurred to the plate, which caused its breast to expand with exultant pride. " Now! I shall soon be out of this kitchen and

into the dining-room." But, oh, how mistaken can be
the most reasonable expectations! The pudding, being properly prepared, was tied up in a clean linen
bag, and the cook (abstractedly perhaps) lifted the
prostrate plate and lowered it to the bottom of a large
black pot. In its descent a harsh, grating *shrick* was
heard, which changed to a violent contest between the
plate and the boiling water, sounding like mumblings
and poundings and thumpings and jumpings. The
ironware fraternity averred that the *shrick* was made
by the pot, but I affirm that it was the shriek of despair from the sinking plate. The revulsion of feeling
consequent upon the dining-room disappointment and
the dismay and helplessness while struggling in the
boiling waves, confirm me in this conclusion. Pots, especially iron pots, are dull objects, devoid of that more
refined organization of the plate family, and are used
to the boiling process. However, the weight of the
fine fruit-pudding soon settled the struggle, and, after
a lapse of a few moments, the lid was lifted up and
down evenly to the tune of the delicate steam. Three
hours of this terrible ordeal passed, unrealized by the
kitchen occupants except only as the proper period
of time requisite for the cooking of the pudding. Then,
with alacrity of movement and the liveliest expressions
of solicitude (for the well-being of the pudding), the
cook's assistant lifted the steaming, odorous mass
into the platter held in obsequious waiting, and whereon
it was conveyed with all due haste to the broad table,
and there liberated from the strained and almost burst-

ing linen which had bound it.   After a critical inves-
tigation by the kitchen autocrat, consisting of several
delicate piercings with golden broom straws, and professional sniffings of the delectable vapors which surrounded its corpulent proportions, a second and grander
platter was ordered, and, being produced with promptitude, the pudding was relegated thereto, and carried
with much dignity and suitable accessions to the dining-room.   The little scullery-maid now proceeded
with a skimmer to lift out the plate from the bottom
of the pot, when, to her surprise, she found that it was
cracked almost its diameter, and, despite the delicate
sighs that rose from its o'erclouded face, she carried it
out and dumped it into the ignoble ash receptacle, and
then returned as though nothing extraordinary had
occurred.   The little maid then washed the dishes that
encumbered the large table, and, having finished, solil-
oquized: " I always liked this little dish-cloth, and I'm
going to wash it clear from suds and hang it among
the roses to dry."

That evening when the portly cook was putting
away the extra silver tablespoons used that day, she
spied something through the open window and took
it in, saying : "I'm going to lay this clean linen cloth
on top of these ; it is so white and soft and nice, and
I don't care about its being worn all to pieces ; it is
nearly as fine as a napkin."

From amid the ashes which nearly smothered and
blinded the forgotten plate, these words of the cook
were heard, and the tender touches of her hands observed.

Too broken in strength to struggle for assistance, to make an appeal or whisper a farewell, the plate, after watching the little locked box of spoons carried from the kitchen to the dining-room safe, sank back among the ashes and was seen no more amid its former associates. But so long as this narrator remained where these incidents occurred, the unpretending dish-cloth retained its place of promotion among the family silver.

A Scene of Early Days

Out of their peaceful slumbers
  The little children woke,
When the tramp of armed and angry men
  The night's deep silence broke.
And, shuddering, they listened to
  The threatened doom they swore,
And their father's step, as he rose to meet
  The mobbers at his door.

'Twas cold, and dark the night looked,
  But colder, darker yet
The hearts and faces of the men
  The Mormon father met.
Many a month of hardship,
  Many a sleepless night,
While the hungry cried, and his dear ones clung
  Around him in their fright,

Had worn his strength to weakness,
  . And now he stood at bay,
A hunted soul—and in despair
  Heard what they had to say:
"Bring out your Mormon children!
  Nor dare our word defy,
For we are firm, and the oath is sworn
  That you and they must die."

No anger kindled in his eye;
  His cheek was wan and thin;
But pity melted not their hearts,
  As he went slowly in.
The feeble candle threw its light
  Upon the door-yard bare—
Shone on their rifles, steely cold-
  Their stern eyes' evil glare.

He spread a quilt before them,
  Then, from the lowly bed,
Without a kiss, without a word,
  Lifted each little head.
In his true arms he bore them,
  And, 'neath the midnight sky,
Placed one by one his children dear
  Before their God to die!

And standing 'mid them, faithful,
  With bared and reverent head,
"Now, shoot them if God will let you,"
  Were all the words he said.
The mobbers looked in each other's eyes;
  Not one had voice to say
The answering word, but each one turned
  And silent rode away.

From hate and power of mobbers
   Their guiltless lives were spared;
Their steps were led through desert paths,
   And perils wild they dared.
Then followed years of peace and joy,
   Of plenty and sweet rest—
His children's children throng his home,
   His name is honored, blest.

But hark! his soul so long on watch,
   Hath caught a far-off sound—
The foeman's step; oppressions might
   Approach our rightful ground.
O Father, reach out thine arm again,
   Thy children still to save;
Make strong thy hosts, thy banners bid
   O'er all thy temples wave.

Jimmy.

JIMMY was about thirteen years old. He lived in a tenement house on a very narrow and dusty street, rarely traveled by any but delivery-wagons, butcher-carts, and such like, and the front-door view was of other people's back premises.

His parents were poor; his father worked away from home months at a time, coming home for the holidays—Fourth of July and Christmas—and of all the year these were the best and happiest days for

Jimmy; for then his father gave his only boy a little spending money, and once a suit of ready-made clothing, with twenty-five cents in the right-hand pants pocket.

His mother, too, went out by the day; and though I used to think she really loved Jimmy best of all (because he was a boy), still she always provided for his sisters first, because persons notice little girls' clothing, and they had to look neat at school. By the time she had attended to their wants, and it came Jimmy's turn, generally the money was all gone, or the rent was just due, or her husband's remittance had failed to arrive on time, and a bill of credit was accumulating; all these, and perhaps other conditions, so intervened between her intentions and her actual performance of them, that it became quite the common thing for Jimmy to be the neglected and poorest-dressed member of the family.

"Boys don't mind about their looks as girls do." "Nobody notices how boys look." "They're always down on their knees playing marbles, and good clothes would soon look just as bad," is the style in which neglect of boys' appearance and comfort is often excused.

Now Jimmy did love to see his little sisters look neat and pretty on their way to school, and did not envy them a ruffle on their aprons, or even buttoned shoes when laced shoes would have done just as well and would have been a saving towards his wardrobe; and when his mother bought some little extra for herself, so as to look nice when she went to work for fine persons, Jimmy thought she looked prettier than ever.

But when he started down town to hunt a day's work or some errand to do, and instinctively looked at his limp felt hat, shabby overalls, and grimy hands, then at his bare toes, I know Jimmy had a very downcast and abstracted air, and a general lack of confidence in anyone wanting to give him anything to do.

But, happily, boys are liable to sudden changes of feeling, and the first "Hello, Jim!" that greeted him had power to rout instantly every dark thought, and set him on good terms with all the world again, and the two or three would set off together in quest of something to do. Boys who were apprenticed to trades ventured generous and impossible suggestions to do as they were doing, but the superintendents always had "boys enough at present," which "present" time seemed to be all the year round.

These more fortunate boys all liked Jimmy, and when coasting was in season he was always among them, apparently as happy as any. They divided their treats of candy, etc., with him, and played marbles or kite as enjoyably with him as with any other boy. On the occasion of a circus, I am happy to say that Jimmy was always seen going in with the crowd of his friends, and I have even known several of them to accompany him after their work-hours to the rear of some store (by permission) in quest of discarded boxes for kindling-wood.

These expeditions were made with great zeal, and intense enthusiasm prevailed when the search resulted in such discoveries as swept-out sticks of gum, "charm buttons," cracked pocket-mirrors, old lead-pencils, etc, the spoils being always honorably divided, though often into painfully small portions.

Sometimes the boxes (always acknowledged to be Jimmy's property) would be pronounced too good for kindling-wood. An exchange for rougher material would ensue, with liberal "boot" thrown in, such as "flipper 'lastic," "pearl-handled knife with only three blades gone," the incomplete works of a nickel-cased watch, or a pocket-pistol no longer dangerous. How I have listened and laughed at their bartering under the fence, and how they took satisfaction!

When Jimmy's mother came home tired enough, and smiled to see the fire he had ready, and the little girls getting the table set, didn't he feel that he had done his share? Perhaps he had worked part of the day, and invested in a bologna sausage; or, yielding to temptation, made a reckless expenditure in small cakes and caramels enough for a taste all around; or, if he had been completely unfortunate all day, and came home with a heavy heart, whichever way it was, be sure his mother gave him her fondest smile, and had most to say to Jimmy.

Their rooms were small and uncomfortably warm in summer, and very muddy about the door in winter. But the mother had a knack of making such pretty tidies for stands and shelves, and the cheap white muslin curtains, trimmed with her own crochet lace, draped the windows so prettily, and the cook-stove shone so brightly, that the plain rooms looked quite cheerful.

In the evenings, as the mother sewed or crocheted, she told them stories of the farm their father once owned, of the cow she milked, the plenty of sweet milk, good butter, and green corn, "roasting ears." Jimmy listened, and a longing grew in his heart to go into the country and live just such a life. He made many resolves to go and work with his father as soon as his mother would consent, and by his help they would all the sooner own a piece of land, a cow and calf—he would train the calf himself—and a horse. How his heart swelled at the very hope! Then, thought he, how happy he would be to have all the boys come out to their place and see his pets and eat melons! And how he would show them where to find bird'snests, squirrels, and rabbits! And what rambles they would all take under his leadership!

This all seemed only a matter of time to Jimmy, and he forgot many of his present troubles in happy day-dreams. If Jimmy sometimes said, "May be our folks will move out onto a farm some time," the boys had no doubt of it, and cheerfully hoped it might happen soon, so they would all have somewhere to go and visit. The discussion of the matter seldom went further; for wasn't Jimmy's father a miner? And how was anybody to know but that he was economically and steadily putting aside enough to sometime

very soon buy a modest little farm, with complete
outfit ?

The hard winter had gone, spring-time and sore
throats were disappearing, and on sunny days shoes
and stockings could be dispensed with; the sidewalks
were in good condition for marble playing, and the
wind on the hill was not too rough for kite flying—
altogether, life was easing a little for Jimmy. He was
having less anxiety about kindling-wood, and could
devote some time to gathering water-cress and dande-
lions, which "brought in the nickels if boys would
just go around to folks' houses with their baskets."
A rather novel feature of this kind of traffic was that
several boys went together to each house, and by the
abundance thus exhibited seemed to depress trade
rather than the reverse; and sometimes the housekeeper was in perplexity which party to patronize, out
of delicate regard for individual feelings.   When I
once ventured to suggest a different arrangement to
the boys, I learned that this combination of interests
was necessary to engender sufficient confidence to
carry on the business, and that they "divided turns"
in selling, or receiving money, by an arrangement
equally profitable all around.

Just as Jimmy was doing fairly well and beginning
to see a definite prospect of a new hat and overalls, he
became sick.   It was not considered anything serious
at first—only a sore throat—and by his mother's wish
Jimmy stayed at home all day to take care of himself
and be ready for the next day's campaign.   When his

mother came home at night, he had a fever. The boys came around the gate, and finally sent in word that they would come that way in the morning. By the time they appeared, Jimmy was helpless with a burning fever, and they went on in a lingering, unsatisfied manner for a block or two, then stopped to talk it over, arriving at an arrangement to sell one or two baskets to Jimmy's customers for him, and call and report financially. This resolve had great effect in elating their spirits, and inspiring great diligence in the forenoon's work and the afternoon's sales. But when they filed up the steep, narrow sidewalk and neared the house, a yellow flag, the sign of diphtheria, floated from over the door. A swift exchange of surprised looks, a brief consultation, and then one of them said, "I don't care, I'll take his money to the door anyway."

The rest of the group stood with cautious prudence quite near enough to catch the infected atmosphere, and watched the bearer approach the door, and, putting the money into the bewildered mother's hand, then deliver a brief explanation.

"I'll put it by till he can understand, and then tell him," she said; "but he's very sick, the doctor says." And the poor mother brushed her hand across her eyes, and turned to answer Jimmy's faint, delirious call.

Very quietly the boys walked away, and halted at the corner instead of making their usual visit to a baker's shop.

"Poor Jimmy! I guess, though, he'll get well, don't you think so?" "Let's come up this way in the morning. I've got a pup I was going to give Jimmy," said another. "I wish water-melons were ripe, I think one might do him good," added a third. "And I'll tell my mother, she knows what's good for sickness—jellies and things," joined in the fourth. This last suggestion seemed to afford more immediate satisfaction than the others, and they parted, each going his own way at quickened pace to tell the news at home that "Jimmy Jones has got the diphtheria, the very worst kind. It's so, I've been right to the house."

This communication was received with unmistakable interest and alarm in each home where it was repeated, and painful injunctions given as to the next day's appointed visit.

Watching so eagerly for a return of consciousness in the sufferer's face, sat the sorrowful mother. He called her, he seemed to know her all the time, and she caught the chance to try and bring back other memories.

"Jimmy, dear, the boys were here last night. They brought your share of money for the water-cress; see, here it is, won't you hold it in your hand?"

He looked at her, and she knew he thought only of her; the poor brown fingers that she had shut upon the two dimes and the two nickels opened, and the unnoticed silver rolled upon the white sheet. She picked them up again and held them so that he could see them: "The boys brought you this, Jimmy, they said it was yours; look, dear."

But Jimmy only answered, "Mother, take me." And her tired, loving arms that had lifted and held him night and day, raised him up again, so that he would cease his restless moving and moaning.

The hot sun came through the white curtains; the smell of stale water and soap-suds thrown out upon the little yards of the tenement houses came in through the raised windows; the flies swarmed in, too, and the air was full of kitchen odors and medicines. The low wall, where hung his faded and frayed apparel, faced him; the low, smoky ceiling seemed to close down upon him; voices from all through the house reached that room, and dust rolled in from the street; and if any remembrance of earthly ills or happy plans he had told came back to him, or if a better promise, a truer and sweeter, was before his eyes, that looked with so uncertain gaze in hers, she could not tell.

The father sat in helpless silence looking on the wasted form; the children tiptoed carefully about with whispers and tearful eyes; and, alive to all, caring for everything, for nothing, shuddering, with one dreadful truth before her, yet holding back the cry of anguish struggling to be free, the mother held him to her heart, and watched the last look answer to her own, heard the last breath pass away forever—and Jimmy was gone!

To a Child.

Amy, dear child, of all thy friends
    Prize first and best thy mother;
Her love for thee would still live on
    Though changed were every other.
Thy youthful mind not now can judge
    Its depth, and worth, and beauty;
Life's lessons and life's years alone
    Can teach thy debt and duty.

Then follow where her counsels lead—
    True mothers ne'er guide wrongly—
Gather her teachings to thy heart,
    And therein bind them strongly.
And let thy father's memory,
    With hers, light thine ambition,
To fill in like integrity
    Life's every worthy mission.

The friendships that we prize to-day
    Are but as beacons, leading
To sweeter years and holier love,
    If we God's words are heeding.
Shouldst thou e'er search in memory's hour
    Earth's truest friends—no others—
Thy lone heart may be sure of these:
    Thy father's and thy mother's.

Silent Influences.

Upon a few occasions during my goings back and forth in Utah, I have observed some little things that I have often since reflected upon.

It is an idea that a mother's influence is most appreciated when years of mature reflection come, and that that influence is apparent more to the family than to anyone else, but I know that there have been mothers who, being dead, have yet spoken to strangers by tokens beyond praise of tongue or pen.

Upon one occasion while traveling southward to visit my parents, the person whom I had hired to take me on my journey, to my surprise, stopped at a poor log house and asked for accommodations, which the man consented to in a hesitating way I did not understand. I went into the house with my three little ones, and, being surrounded by little strangers, I knew there must be a mother. At last I inquired for her.

The largest girl, about eleven years of age, and who was holding the baby of one year, answered, " Ma has been dead three weeks."

" And who takes care of the children ? " I asked.

" Me and pa."

" But the house-work, my poor little girl ? "

" We do it; my ma never hired help."

I thought that the best thing for me to do was to help get the supper instead of letting that little girl wait on me, and by her assistance, and showing where things were, we had as cozy a time as I could have with the sad thoughts that would keep coming up behind all our talk. Such little interruptions and breaks in our talks as, "Oh, yes, that's how ma used to do it! I don't always remember just how she used to tell me to do things, and now sometimes I'm troubled so, not remembering, and the children have to be watched, too."

When supper-time came, the father looked surprised and pleased. "Well, daughter, I'm right proud you've done so well for this lady."

But the daughter could not keep quiet with the honors.

That night when I helped her put four sleepy little ones to bed, I noticed the pretty, hand-made lace on the little night-gowns and the pillow-slips; the patch-work quilts made of such tiny pieces, some of them home-dyed; the flannel underwear all her own spinning and weaving, and some of the little stockings not yet worn through where she had last darned them. I saw patches that I knew a practiced hand had sewed, so even and neat were they; and the bleached muslin window curtains and shelf tidies all trimmed with hand-made lace.

"I know what you're looking at. Ma made that lace; I can see her do it yet, just as plain; that was when she was resting."

The milk was brought in and attended to. "We milk fourteen cows. Pa milks them now. Ma was just as well as ever; she was always tired, though;

and she got cold and had pneumonia and died in four days. I wish you could have seen my ma, you don't know what she was like, but she told us children to always be Saints, no matter what."

I could not help answering: "Yes, dear little girl, all this pretty lace-work, these many quilts and good clothes that her hands made, have told me one by one that she was industrious and looked after the comfort of her family; I see by all your little quiet ways to one another that she was sweet and patient; I know by your words that she was a faithful Saint, and I believe that if she had worked less hard and lived in a comfortable house she would have lived longer."

Tears came in her eyes. "I wish you could stay with us. Father was most ready to put up a good house, and now he says he must."

After breakfast he said to me, "You've taken quite an interest in my little ones, and your medicine did the baby a deal of good during the night; I'd like to show you around, if you'd like it?"

I thanked him and we went out to see the corral full of fat stock, the good orchard, and then the building material and foundation for a good-sized house, all ready to begin. "If I'd only a had this done I don't think she'd have died. The wind always came in through those chinks so, there was no getting out of the draught."

I thought the same, but he seemed so good-hearted about it, I felt as though he was not really to blame, after all. Secretly, and without saying so, I felt all those pretty laces and everything her hands had made enticing me to stay with the children; but my own family and home duties called me along.

An acquaintance had died; and although we had not known each other long, I thought it proper to attend the funeral, which was held at her late home. The children had been given some things to divert their attention, and it was time to gather up these and put them away. As I helped to do so I noticed the character of these every-day playthings, little colored picture-books, and all of them were pretty Bible stories; and on the mantel and bracket shelves were delicate little statuettes of kneeling children, prayerful mothers, and others of like nature. Of the funeral sermon I was particularly impressed by this sentence from one who had known her from girlhood: "It can be said of this sister that she has fulfilled every principle of the gospel as it was made known to her, *without murmuring.*"

" Here," thought I, "has lived one whose example has been as near perfection as is almost possible." And I did not wonder that she was called to a better world.

Upon another occasion a lady said to her guests, " Come, we'll go to the table; all is ready." As we passed from the room, a little child two or three years old ran along with us, and as all were about to seat themselves, they turned with one accord to where the little one had knelt beside a chair. It needed no one to say that the child had been accustomed to daily family prayer.

The Christmas Tithing.

'TWAS near the happy Christmas-time,
  And all the country roads
Were strung along with teams that drew
  Full, high, and plenteous loads,—
The Mormon farmers bringing in
  Their tithing for the year.
Oh, 'twas a sight to cheer the eyes,
  A pleasant sound to hear!

With willing hands they brought to Him
  The tenth of what was given,
And knew His blessing would again
  Unloose the stores of heaven.
The sacks of wheat and flour by which
  The "temple hands" were fed,
The sweet dried fruits and honey-comb,
  And apples, gold and red,
The barrels filled with syrups pure,
  Butter and creamy cheese,
Fluttering poultry—what poor men
  Were ever served like these?

Yet not alone for "temple hands"
  These tithings all were brought, .
In ev'ry ward (ignoring creeds)
  The poor and sad are sought;
Their names are learned, and ev'ry one
  On bishop's list enrolled;
For each are gen'rous baskets filled,

And measured wood and coal;
And busy men step in and out,
As the tithing wagons go
Out through the gate to every ward
Their portion to bestow.

Oh, once I went to many homes,
And happy scenes were they;
There busy worked the wives to get
All done for Christmas-day;
For romping boys were newly made
Full suits of Provo goods;
For little girls, light woolen plaids,
And pretty home-made hoods!

I saw the laborer's sickly child
With dainty food was fed,
As fresh and pure as e'er before
The epicure was spread.
No happier driver takes a load,
Where'er the things may go,
Than he who carries to the poor
On Christmas eve—through snow—
For well he knows how eyes that closed
Expecting naught, shall wake
And find a joyous Christmas gift,
And bless him for its sake.

The many blessings tithing brings
Not you or I can count;
The little tenth from each one swells
To rich and large amount.
Oh, blessings on the heart that gives

The duty that it owes,
And praise His love who made the law.
   That like a river flows
Through all our mountains and our vales,
   Relieving, first, the poor,
And writes the giver's name in lines
   Forever shall endure!

A Dialogue on the Book of Mormon.

[Written by request of Sister Rebecca W. Brown, of South Bountiful, for her Sunday-school class.]

Hattie—Well, girls, as we shall have a pleasant afternoon all together, how shall we best spend it? I think we had best consult each other and then decide upon doing some one thing and giving it our whole attention. What do you say?

(All reply, " Yes.")

Hattie—Jennie, you are the eldest, what is your idea?

Jenny—Shall we form an industrial committee, take out our thimbles and do up all your sewing—carpet-rags, patchwork or anything else?

Hattie—Oh, no indeed! thank you. Suppose we take up some subject of mental and spiritual improvement. Now for your idea, Laura?

Laura—Well, a great deal has been said about women voting. Shall we discuss that?

Hattie—That is suggestion number two. We'll hear from all and then decide by vote. You next, Annie.

Annie—Another prominent and kindred subject is woman's holding public positions of trust and emolument.

Hattie—Suggestion number three. I think perhaps Alice had better act as secretary, and take account of the propositions. What do you say, Ellen?

Ellen—Shall we relate instances we have read or known of women's deeds of heroism, goodness or missionary labors?

Hattie—A vast subject, indeed! Alice, it is your turn.

Alice—The choice of our literature is, I think, a very important topic; also the present crusade against our religion.

Hattie—Very true, indeed. Ruth, you are the last; what do you suggest?

Ruth—We have heard subjects sufficient presented to engage our minds and hearts upon many future occasions of our girlish gatherings or visits, all of which are worthy and profitable to us as daughters of Zion. I do not wish to press my own idea as better than either, but I had been thinking that I would like to hear some remarks from each of you upon that book so important to us—the Book of Mormon.

Hattie—It seems as though we might well meet often hereafter and devote our serious thoughts to each of these themes; it is easy to discern that much good might result. We will begin by selecting the one for to-day. Jenny can present either one for our vote.

Jenny—The Book of Mormon.

(All hands raised.)

Hattie—A clear vote. Now, I would like to hear which part of the book each one thinks the most interesting, and this will give us an opportunity to learn from each other. Do you agree?

All—Oh, yes!

Jenny—I think that the bringing forth of the Book of Mormon; the history of its concealment and of the youth whom God raised up from obscurity to perform the great latter-day work; the miracle of its translation; the prophetic vision of its result, and the thrilling record of the Prophet Joseph and his brother, are all as interesting as the book itself, and are as a part of it. The testimonies of the three witnesses and also of the eight witnesses are of inestimable value. Many of our parents knew these persons to be good and true men, whose word could not be doubted, and their first testimony to all the world remained unrevoked to their latest day, notwithstanding all the opposition that has been arrayed against the work.

Hattie—Your observations are a fitting preface to

4

the subject. I have often considered the fact that we have no living witnesses to the Bible's authenticity, as in the case of the Book of Mormon, although we honor and reverence the Bible as the undoubted word of God, and the light of all the world.

Laura—I think that the departure of Lehi and his family from Jerusalem, then his obtaining possession of the record of the Jews; their travels, the vision of Lehi, and the wonderful manner in which the Lord conveyed him and his family across the water, to mention no more, all are more deeply interesting and wonderful than any production of any worldly pen that I have any knowledge of.

Annie—I think that the history of the two thousand young men who went with Helaman, is a lesson which should inspire all who read it with firmer faith and trust in God and his servants, for what God has done once he can do again, if we have similar faith, courage and integrity. How I hope that our brothers may prove as noble if the same test comes to them!

Ellen—I love to read of that great general, Helaman, how he resisted the enemy while his own army was small and suffering for food, and faint with long service and exhaustion; and how he nobly waited in patience and hope for help, even while he was grieved and feared his people would be overcome; and then when he had won possession of the city of Manti and could receive no word from the parent government, think how grandly still he "held the fort" in faith and loyalty. He was indeed a grand general!

Julia—And his brother Moroni. What a noble letter he wrote to Pahoran, the governor, and how joyfully he went to Pahoran's relief, and what a grand work they accomplished, re-establishing peace and righteousness in all the land!

Alice—Is it not wonderful that the greatest war recorded in history is written in the Book of Mormon, and took place on our continent?

Ruth—I think the most beautiful part of the book is where Jesus showed himself to the people of Nephi in the land of Bountiful, and how they prevailed upon Him to return to them when He would have passed from their sight. Let us live so that when He comes again we, too, may behold His face and receive the same joy.

And now that we have all had something to say on the subject, and it will soon be time for us to part for this day, I would like to ask if we have not been interested and benefited by our interchange of thought upon the Book of Mormon?

All—Yes.

Alice—Girls, let us make it a rule in our visits to converse upon such themes, striving to gain treasures of wisdom and eternal happiness.

Hattie—As a class and as dear friends, let us keep this in mind, and sometimes let our gathering be around our dear Sunday-school teacher, who has done so much to lead our thoughts in the right way.

All—That's a clear vote!

"The Sabbath Breaker."

ONCE there lived, long years ago,
 A man who sought a wide renown,
Not as philanthropist or divine,
 But as "wickedest man in all the town."
He builded houses strong and high,
 Not for the poor to dwell therein,
But with doors and windows lettered o'er,
 Luring the weak to taste of sin.
Warm and glowing, the great lights burned,
 When the winter winds outside blew cold,
And, while feebly the poor toiled on for dimes,
 O'er his counters glittered the shining gold.
For there, when the week's long toil was done,
 Drawn as by cords, did the laborer come
And spend, while his dear ones wept at home,
 His hard-earned wages at last for *rum*.
There, while the timid hurried past,
 They heard the drunkard's wildest song,
And oft above it the gambler's oath,
 Or the deadly shot in the outcast throng.

Nor woman's prayer, nor children's tears,
 Nor scenes of suff'rings howe'er deep,
Could turn his heart from its wicked course,
 Or trouble in dreams his heavy sleep.
But, unsatisfied yet, his darkened mind
 Searched long and deep for some further ill,
To affront, by power of might and gold,
 To flaunt the strength of his evil will.

"The Sabbath Breaker."

At last, one beautiful Sabbath morn,
  Into his sinful mind there came,
Like a guilty thing, a new-born plan
  With hate and wickedness aflame.
He sought and gathered out dark-souled men,
  To fill the contract his mind had planned,
To build a boat, all by Sabbath work,
  To defy the day, and the Lord's command.
It filled his soul with an evil joy,
  When passers paused, at the hammer's sound.
Oh, louder and worse their discord seemed,
  In the quiet elsewhere all around!
But the work went on till the boat was done,
  Painted, the flag made, too; then came
Into his heart a further task—
  The search for a fitting, evil name.
'Twas found!   On the red and yellow flag
  That idly streamed above his head,
In letters of black, like a venomed sting—
  He smiled, and "THE SABBATH BREAKER" read.

Not till another Sabbath morn
  Was the dark boat launched—an evil sight!
Just as the throngs of children sweet
  Walked, in the sunshine warm and bright,
With loving parents and teachers good,
  From ev'ry street to the house of prayer,
Dismayed, they saw the new-launched boat—
  Heard the drunken song on the holy air.

And then, as the evil men had timed,
  When the Sabbath-schools poured forth their throngs,
Again they heard, o'er the waters clear,

The returning sinners' ribald songs.
And just above, o'er their reckless heads,
  A small black cloud in the sky arose.
On land they shuddered, and they at sea
  Turned to the shore ere the storm should close
O'er their helpless heads. But drunken, weak,
  In vain they strove; the Almighty's wrath
By His lightnings pierced, by His thunders spoke,
  And towering billows checked their path.
The sudden winds roared o'er their cries,
  The torrent rains swept o'er their deck,
And when the furious tempest passed,
  They who looked forth to see the wreck
Saw, through the mists not yet quite cleared,
  And where the billows last had raved,
Rose a broken mast, o'er the buried crew,
  Where the flag, "THE SABBATH BREAKER," waved.

Tithing and Fast=day Offerings.

LITTLE Bessie Lane lived in Salt Lake City, in
rather comfortable circumstances, her father being a
clerk in a large mercantile establishment. Bessie had
two brothers and one little sister, so she had companions enough for play, study, or working hours. Bessie's mother was industrous, and never a seamstress or
other hired help was engaged except in rare cases, for
the mother wished her children to learn all useful home
employments. They rented a plain cottage with a

small garden and a few trees, and this set them often
to wishing that they owned a home of their own, so that
they might plant for future as well as present interests;
they often, also, expressed their wishes to own a cow,
a horse, and some chickens, and imagined how hard
they would work if such could only be their good-
fortune in life. Their mother once told them that
God had promised to grant all our reasonable desires
if we would obey His commandments and seek His
throne by daily, earnest prayer, and they began to
try to fulfill their part of the conditions with sincere
faith, from that very time.

One morning in September their mother asked
Bessie and Harry to carry down to the Tithing Office a peck basket of pears. They had always made
it a practice to pay the tithing at the end of the year
in money, but on this occasion Mrs. Lane concluded
to send these fine pears. Bessie looked unwillingly
at the basket and replied, "Why not let pa pay the
money instead, as he always does."

And Harry answered, "I don't ever see boys taking
things in baskets to the Tithing Office."

Mrs. Lane replied: "I have been thinking how the
law of tithing used to be, that we should pay our
tithing on just what we earn, or raise, or make; and
if others for convenience or some other reason do differently, that is nothing to justify us from obeying the
plain word of the Lord, especially when we can do so
as well as not. So go, and perhaps you will learn a
lesson."

Bessie and Harry each took hold of the basket handle and went down street rather seriously. When Bessie returned, her eyes were brighter, and she was in haste to tell her story. "O ma, you've no idea how pleased the man was to see those pears. He said they were the first ones brought in this season, and gave us credit on the book for seventy-five cents. Who would have expected that? Then a man stepped up and said, 'I'll take the lot, if you please,' and the clerk said, 'No, these must be divided so as to go as far as possible; you can have three, if you want.' The man took three and then another one said, 'I would like three, I have a sick child;' and a young girl said, 'I would like some too, for my poor old grandma,' and while we stood there every pear was given out, and, O ma, I wish there had been a bushel instead of a peck."

"Ma," said Harry, "I'm glad you had the word of the Lord right in your head; just see how good it turned out."

"Yes, children, the Lord knows just which is the best way of doing everything, and when He is kind enough to teach us, we should be willing to obey."

After this the children were very anxious to keep account and take a full and correct tithing of all the little garden afforded, and were very happy when one day the clerk said: "You little children are the most regular, prompt and best tithing payers in this department. Everything is so clean and fresh and you come as if it were a treat to you to bring it."

One fast-day morning, instead of taking some silver

change, as had been her custom, Mrs. Lane filled the basket with small parcels,—sweet, fresh butter, packages of rice, sugar and raisins, and some ham, just what she would have used that day for her own family. Bessie and Harry looked at each other but said nothing, even when Annie, the eldest sister, said, "That basket looks so conspicuous and old-fashioned, too."

After the meeting was over, Mrs. Lane went a little farther on, to the Bishop's house, with her basket. As the Bishop's wife took out the things, she remarked pleasantly: "How nice these will be for that sick family, and will save our going down town after these very articles! This bunch of grapes will be delightful to the poor woman's fevered taste." Some general conversation then ensued and Mrs. Lane returned home.

A few weeks later Mr. Lane was taken sick and on his recovery could not go back to the store; his place had been filled, and in vain he strove to obtain another. By a dispensation of providence he was enabled to exchange some mining stock for a small house in the suburbs of the city, and thither the family moved. One cow and a few chickens, with a few fruit-trees and scant vegetable garden, afforded part of their sustenance; and, one by one, they were obliged to part w   les of value to get shoes, coal and light. Unable now to pay for their schooling, they kept their children at home to study alone as best they could.

Times grew harder month after month, until even the visiting "teachers" felt prompted to offer assistance. It would be difficult to imagine their distress of spirit when they were at last compelled to accept charity; they who were all willing to work if work could only be had.

Doubtless the Lord had His own reasons for bringing them into this state, and they did not murmur against Him, but constantly implored Him to open their way before them, feeling all the time that they would rather endure even worse than this than turn away from the faith.

It was arranged that the fast-day offerings should all be given to the family of Mr. Lane, they being the only ones in that particular district in special need. In some way the matter became known, and little Bessie's cheeks and eyes were often wet with tears of mortification.

One day her father came home with some flour and meat. "Pa, don't folks down here ever bring anything for fast offerings but flour and meat? Don't you think some syrup or fruit would taste good?"

"Dear child," he answered, "I expect they don't think of it as you do. We must be thankful for flour, until I can get work. Then you shall have syrup and many other comforts."

Bessie's mother drew her darling to her side and whispered: "If we are prospered again, do you think you have got the law of tithing and of the fast-day offerings securely committed in your mind?"

And Bessie, pale-faced and grieving, sweetly answered, "Yes, ma, and in my heart."

"Do you think you would have learned and understood these laws of God as well if we had not been placed as we are now? No, daughter, those lessons He desires to engrave deeply upon our hearts must be written there by experience alone, and when, in His time, we are blessed with his bounties, let us do as we did before, and, with generous measure, pay these dues to the poor, in kind, of everything we enjoy, and with never-changing humility of spirit."

Bessie answered with a kiss, and turned to her supper of bread and milk, accepting the lesson of life from God with sweetness, patience and faith.

The Twenty-Fourth.

"GRANDPA, what is the Twenty-fourth,
  That's coming so soon, they say?
Who made it, and what was it made about,
  To be such a splendid, happy day?"

Then over the face of the gray-haired man
  A thoughtful expression came,
That lit his cheek with a sudden flush
  And his eye like a quickened flame,
And he lifted up to his knee and breast
  The darling six-year-old,
Silent a moment, while through his mind
  The hurrying visions rolled.

Then first he told of the Pilgrim band,
  And the barren Plymouth shore,
With the cruel Indian foe behind
  And the stormy sea before.

THE TWENTY-FOURTH.

Of the weary years of toil and fear
  Before they dwelt at ease;
And then how a tyrant's cruel might
  Reached them even across the seas;
And how they covered the new-made graves
  All over with wheat-fields green—
Their lessened numbers these would have shown,
  Could the Indian foe have seen.

And then he told how the king shut off
  The ships with the sugar trade,
And how the Pilgrims at Boston Bay
  Of the ocean a tea-pot made.
Then many a battle followed fast,
  And many a noble name,
Marquis' and count's and baron's too,
  With our generals linked their fame;
How the words that Patrick Henry spoke
  Like martial music rolled,
And his eye grew moist, when the suffering
  At Valley Forge was told;
But when he told of Bunker Hill,
  And Marion's noble men,
Of Lord Dacie's and Lord Cornwallis' defeats,
  His eye grew bright again.
"At last," said grandpa, "they threw off
  The English monarch's yoke,
And when the independence bell
  Its peal of freedom spoke,
Oh, never upon the broad, green earth
  Were happier men than they,
For their work was built upon God's own rock,
  To last upon earth alway !

"Then 'neath its shelter and its care
    It pleased our God to raise
Another work of nobler kind
    To his own glorious praise.
A perfect government he gave
    To bless the homes of men,
And then the gospel's plan to link
    High heaven with earth again.

"But, oh, the hearts of men forgot
    Whence all their rights were won,
And they oppression's power revived
    Ere seventy years had gone!

"Our honored patriot fathers' names
    Our country still reveres,
But *Joseph's* name they wrote in blood
    And in his people's tears.

"Then, like the Puritans of old,
    The Saints left all behind,
And crossed the trackless deserts wild,
    New homes and peace to find.
Here, too, the Indian foe they met,
    Famine and pain and cold;
Here, too, oppression followed them,
    With greed and hate untold.

"Twas on July the Twenty-fourth
    The resting-place was found.
The Great Salt Lake spread out ahead,
    And mountains walled them round.
Then *Brigham* knew the sacred spot,

And saw with prophet's eyes
A splended city; in its midst
A glorious temple rise.
He saw on barren Ensign's height
Our country's flag float free—
And gave the word to plant it there
' For God and Liberty.'

"Long years they dwelt in sweet content,
And as the years came round,
The ' Fourth' and then the ' Twenty-fourth'
With honors due were crowned.
Such grand parades as then we had!
The guns could scarce grow cold
Before we had them out again
And all the past retold.

" But then there came a governor
Who stopped our loudest fun,
And what is Independence-day
When boys can't fire a gun?
I'll tell you what it seemed to me
Just like the ' Fourth' was dead.
Of course, we played the same old tunes
And the *Constitution* read;
But when the flag snaps in the breeze
To the martial music's sound,
And we've got the spirit of ''76'
We went the cannon 'round.

" But stop, who is't I'm ta'king to ?
These little Mormon boys,
Who've never heard, and never missed,

The good old times and noise;
They look with wondering eyes on me,
    As though some legend old
Had fired my brain and loosed my tongue
    That were so still and cold.

"But I tell you, grandsons all of mine,
    Listen, and don't forget,
We'll have the old 'Fourth' and the 'Twenty-fourth,'
    And the cannon with them yet.

"We'll have the brave 'Battalion Boys'
    And the 'Nauvoo Legion' too,
And will sing the old-time Mormon songs
    Just as we used to do.

"Now, Johnny, slide from off my knee
    And stand up in my chair,
I've got three cheers that I want to ring
    On the hushed and empty air.
Three cheers for our country and her flag,
    The best, the dearest still;
Three cheers for our Rocky Mountain home
    And the Saints—let come what will.
Three cheers for the time when, East and West,
    From the South to the frozen North,
We may sing and pray in our temples free,
    'Neath our flag, on our 'Twenty-fourth.'"

5

The Mother's Heart.

IF children could realize how indifference and disrespect to parents wound the heart, they would never
offend in that way. "Honor thy father and thy
mother," is one of the first commands, and was intended to be obeyed as much as any other. When
one of God's commands is disobeyed, a penalty is
sure to follow, whether the transgressor realizes
the cause or not. It may be that every disappointment, loss, sickness or affliction is a penalty merci-
fully appointed to pay the debt here instead of hereafter. If so, what a load we would carry with us
into the next life to our great shame and hindrance
if we do not expiate, in part, our faults while here.

If a person should make you a costly present, you
would entertain the most pleasant feelings toward
that one; your countenance would brighten and your
step hasten to do some kindness in return, and this
you would perhaps consider almost nothing in comparison. Yet, to those who gave you the first smile
and welcome, shelter, food and clothing, loving care
and teaching,—do you respond as willingly? If so,
how sweet must be the thought; if not, there will be
much to regret some day.

If you were making some beautiful article for yourself, your time and materials being limited, and you
should mar your workmanship beyond repairing,

how sorrowful you would be; but the spirit and
the record you are moulding are what money cannot
create or replace; neither can time efface from the
faithful records of the heart, the vivid picture of a
misused opportunity, an injured work of the soul.
There is some consolation in the knowledge that
repentance cancels part of the offense, if not its
result; but the heart that never repents or seeks to
amend its wrongs, the heart that fosters ingratitude,
is cultivating an element that will at last destroy
every bright attribute and hope.

Let me tell you a story or two from life to show
you the tenderness of a mother's heart, its long,
enduring love.

A woman past sixty years of age, a tailoress, lived
near me. She had sons and grandchildren, and was
very kind to them all, constantly helping to provide
for the families, and even now and then lending some
poor man or woman a sum of money to start business
with; always cheerful and hopeful in her ways, and
never idle. Early and late her sewing-machine was
hurrying, and some persons hinted that she must
have riches hoarded up. One day a young woman
entered the shop, and the tailoress looking at the
baby she carried in her arms, the baby responded
with a coo and a spring toward her. "What do you
think of my baby? Just take her a minute," said the
young mother. The gray-haired woman drew back,
and a strange look came over her face. "I have
never held a girl-baby in my arms since my own little

girl died—I cannot!" said she. "How long ago was
that?" tenderly asked the young mother. "Thirty
years," answered the poor woman, and the tears
came so fast she had to wipe them away, and the rest
of us had to wipe our eyes too. Long as we had
known her, we had never had a thought that a secret,
beautiful and sacred sorrow was hidden in her heart,
but I know that ever afterward we who were in her
shop that afternoon always spoke with tenderness to
the poor old woman, as though we were partners in
her sorrow.

THE GRAVE AT NEPHI.

There was another old woman, quite an eccentric
person, whom some young folks used to smile at
when she came to their houses with her basket of
lace and other small things; she was so lofty about
her business, as though it were vastly more important
than it really was, and so cheerful about it, as though
it was a very delightful way of making her living.
"I'm sorry you have to earn your living this way,"
said a young lady to her one day. "Why, my dear,
it's just as well as for your father to be selling
furniture the year around; I only has to earn a little
bit for myself, and it brings in all I need, and I gets
acquainted with lots of fine young folks, and I sees
all the pretty things as I pass along as well as if I
was riding, and I gets refreshed a bit, and when I
goes home I've lots to think over that I've seen
through the day, and that's better than sitting alone
and fretting. I'm well off, my dear, to get what I

need and lay a bit by for a future day." We all felt
a little touched, and when she missed coming next
week we hardly knew what to think, but the week
after she came again, and we inquired if she had been
sick. "No, my dears, I have been down to Nephi on
the excursion train to visit my daughter." "Why,
we didn't know you had a child living." "And I
hasn't, my dears; my daughter has been dead and
buried these eighteen years; only nineteen when she
died; and every year I goes down once in the summer
and takes my bouquet of flowers to lay on her grave,
and I has my bread and cheese and bottle of cold tea,
and I sits down by her grave till sundown, and we
has a comfortable time together that lasts till I goes
again."

Do you think we felt like smiling slyly at her odd
ways after that? One of us went out and brought a
tray with refreshments, and never forgot to do the
same thing in all her after calls. She had kept her
Decoration-day years before it had become a na-
tional custom.

Let me tell you of another mother's faithful heart.
This woman had such love for children, such tender
pity for the orphan, that she had, when we first met
her, raised three adopted children of different parent-
age. One day a person said to her, "You never had
a child of your own, did you?" "Yes, I have got a
son of my own," proudly answered the dear old lady.
The questioner paused in surprise, and thought,
"Perhaps she left him for the Gospel's sake," and

respectfully pursued, "Did you leave him in the old country?" "Yes, I have left my dear boy in the old country." "How old is he? and does he write to you?" "He does not write to me; he is twenty-three years old. He died when he was five." "Died? then you have not got him now!" "Yes, I have got him now; I have got him all the time, I have never lose him, he is mine."

Children, let these brief stories prove to you that each heart bears its own hidden, sweet history, and do be careful when meeting the aged, the poor and humble, to speak kindly and show them respect; perhaps this is all you can ever do for them, and you little know what might be revealed to claim your pity and admiration.

Lizzie and Her Mother.

SOME years ago there used to come to my house twice a week a young English girl. From the first day, her quiet manner and gentle spirit interested me. There are many lights and shades of human character. Lizzie was tall and slender, with fair complexion and very large blue eyes that were expressive of tenderness. Her duties for me were of the plainest character, and I thought she did not appear strong enough, so I gently suggested as much, thinking it only fair that she should understand in the beginning and not

undertake what might overtax her strength. Her
answer was so cheerful : " I am sure I can do it, ma'am.
I shan't think of its being hard work, I'll be thinking
of mother and Rufie and trying to do justice to you,
ma'am. It's all in the way of thinking, I believe."
Who could help admiring her straightway? Between
breakfast and dinner I handed her a slight refreshment, and she pleasantly said: " It's like the stile by
the hedge-row; it gives a rest on the way. Thank
you." When the money was paid her, she sped away
so lightly I wondered, for she must have been tired, I
thought. Soon after I learned that Lizzie was employed every day but Sunday, and one morning I told
her there was danger of her breaking down in health.
"I think not, ma'am. I thank my heavenly Father
every night for what He's let me earn, and I ask Him
every morning to give me strength for the day's work,
and He's never failed to help me yet."

One evening, as she was about to start home, she
witnessed a neighbor's child leave the door in temper,
to go away and spend the night. Lizzie looked
thoroughly astonished, and, turning to me, remarked:
" I wouldn't be in that young lady's place, and going
away from home, too ; I never goes to bed without
kissing my mother; we none of us knows what might
happen before morning." " You've got a good
mother, Lizzie." " Yes, ma'am, and I'm glad to work
for her now I'm strong enough ; Rufie's too little, and
since father died mother needs Rufie near by to take
her mind off from mourning in the day-time; she does
enough of that when she thinks him asleep."

Lizzie had a little book in which she kept strict account of her earnings and regularly paid her tithing.

She took a great interest in the Lamanites, and felt sorry because they could not appear neat and clean. I found out that Lizzie had some cakes of toilet soap in the little satchel she always brought her apron in, and, favorable opportunities occurring, she managed to give, by signs, toilet lessons to more than one Indian woman. As the cakes were selected with care as to appearance and perfume, they were accepted in as friendly a spirit as they were given. " Lizzie," said I, "you're a diplomat." " What's that, ma'am ? " I explained. " Well, ma'am, the Scriptures say, ' Be ye wise as serpents and harmless as doves,' and I wouldn't hurt their feelings in their afflictions."

By and by Lizzie married and went to her own home, and I long missed her good and gentle ways.

Three years later she passed on to where the meek, the willing, and the pure in heart rest from their labors and receive their eternal reward in joy and glory awaiting them.

Franz and His Mother.

I ONCE knew a woman whose life was a long record of love and kindness worthy of much praise. Her only son died in infancy, and the happy home became more silent than before his precious presence gladdened it. After a few years of lonely sorrow, her heart so craved the companionship of children that she and her husband adopted an orphan girl-baby. A while after this, a deserted infant was also taken into their hearts and home, and still another was laid at their door one stormy night. This was a boy, and she accepted him in place of her lost son. The good woman labored hard to help her husband maintain them, and if he ever reflected how much farther his means would have gone if used only for his dear wife and himself, and still allowed something to put by for old age, he never spoke of it, but was content to share with the little strangers. Many of his friends had emigrated to America, and they wrote such letters to him, how he could become a land-owner so easily, and soon own cows, horses and other good things, until he decided to follow their advice, and was soon on his way. Soon after his arrival he found work at good wages. Everything seemed like a blessing from the Lord, and he looked forward to so many things, all to be accomplished by his thankful heart and willing hands. One night sickness came upon him, and before he realized his danger, the end was near.

The poor widow, in the firm faith of again meeting her husband, struggled on, doing day's work for the support of the children. Laundress by day and seamstress by night, she toiled on. In a few years the eldest girl went to a home of her own, with her mother's blessing. Although she might have remembered her foster-mother's kindness in many ways she seemed not to think of it. Fruit lay wasting in the large orchard, vegetables in the garden, fowls gathered in flocks around the barn-yard, and fresh eggs lay in plenty in the nests, but neither of these found their way to the little widow's home in the city, though the young wife had many company dinners.

As the second daughter had an opportunity of going out to service in a fine family, with good wages and light work, this was also accepted, but instead of following the example of her foster-parents, she spent her means in attempting to follow the fashions of those who were her superiors in station.

Franz, the youngest, remained at home with the mother, and in due time obtained employment in a store, with promise of advancement if deserving. Feeling independent now that he was earning something, he began to be very indifferent to her requests; this grew to open disrespect, and finally he announced his intention to "do as he pleased."

The kind mother bore all his conduct with patience, continually pouring out her sorrow in prayer to the Father, and pleading that his heart might be changed and return to the principles he had forsaken.

Sometimes Franz would bring home a present, which she would accept with kind expressions, although she knew he would at some other time refer to it vauntingly, but she hoped to win him back in time by unwearying kindness. "When he is older and away from giddy boys, he will repent and be my own dear boy again." But Franz was impulsive and head-

strong, scorned to ask counsel or receive it, and before his mother thought of his being a man, Franz
brought home a wife. All the cares and much work
rested upon the mother, now grown gray and feeble.
Even when a babe came to bless the household, it was
only the poor old mother that realized all about it, but
she welcomed it and seemed to feel paid for all her
trials. The child grew to love her dearly, and this
gave the young parents greater freedom to follow
pleasure's rounds. But a change came at last, so
swiftly and strangely it could not have been antici-
pated. Some friends were coming to-morrow to spend
a day with them, and would not the mother go in the
evening, after the baby was asleep and the work was
all done, and order the pastry, fruits, and confectionery?
Franz could not be bothered with anything so easy
for mother to do, and Anna would have no idea what
to order.

The grandma laid the sleeping infant in his crib, and,
speaking to his parents, "I go now," left the house.
More than an hour had passed, and she was returning
wearily, when—"Oh, was the house on fire?" The
feeble limbs hurried along. The house was reached.
"Franz! Anna!" she called, but met no answer. The
door was unlocked, and she mounted the stairs through
the smoke that came from the bedroom. She found
the crib. Her loved one was there, but now—where
was the door? Was he alive? With the warm
smoke choking her, she called on the Lord to deliver
her for the sake of the little child. A flash of flame

burst up before her and she saw the way. Gathering her skirt around the babe to protect it from tongues of fire, she plunged through and down the steps out into the fresh, cool air at last. And the babe—the sweet air was restoring him; he was alive. "Franz! Anna!" called the mother, but a fireman answered, "They were out walking, listening to the band; were not you at home?" They were soon there, for the cry of fire had spread and echoed down the street. They had left the baby asleep—he always slept so well —and they thought mother would be home soon, and then the lamp must have exploded. So they said, when they found what had happened.

But the poor mother—it was feared that her face and hands would always be scarred; and oh, how Franz wept, and how his heart smote him, for every time he looked upon her bandaged face, the sight pierced him through without mercy, and he could not still the cries of conscience! What did he not owe to her who had reared him when his own parents cast him forth; all those years of labor, love, and example, and then at last she had saved his child from his own wicked carelessness, at the risk of her own life! "Franz, I must better go," she whispered one day, but his sobs frightened her so she put out her hands and found him where he knelt beside her. "Hush! my dear boy, and I will try to stay." If her bandaged eyes could have seen his efforts to control his anguish and remorse! Weeks passed before they looked upon him again, and then the eyes of her soul saw that the answer to her prayers had come at last.

Grandmother's Knitting.

" How still the house seemed on our return, and we felt that all was now done that could be done at present for grandmother! The great arm-chair in the cozy place between the center-table and fire-place, how solemn it looked; and the head-rest, one could not help touching it gently—her silvery head would never rest against it any more! How lonely it all was!

" Who was there now for the noisy boys to rush to with their wonderful statements of what had been done by themselves? Where should wee Dollie go now for comfort and that comprehension of all her little troubles that came by an intuition, almost inspiration, in grandma? Who would now kindly interpose between the offender and justice with the authoritative assurance that ' they didn't mean anything wrong, it was all an accident'? Whose kindly interventions passed unresented by parental powers like grandma's? Whose 'bless you!' was so implicitly valued as hers? and whose kisses so comforting? No one else could draw out a splinter or tie up a cut finger like her, and what an inexhaustible store of things needful she always had convenient enough, when nobody else could find anything in the hurry! Who was it divided up their share of the nuts and hard candies with the members who had sound teeth? How she always praised those teeth and the red lips of the lit-

tle ones, without the slightest particle of envy! Who
ever knew a grandma to envy her dear ones anything
in this wide world, even when she was deprived of
those same blessings herself? Who ever forgave
faults, even when repeated, like grandma? And as to
story-telling, anyone knows that she could tell better
ones than anyone else, and you always felt as though
they were all true. And her singing! what if her voice
wavered and she would stop and say, 'Children, I
can't sing!' what an utter rejection the very idea received. Grandma not sing, indeed! You couldn't
find anyone else who suited so well. It was lots better
than that high-flight, scientific singing you had to keep
so awful still about. Ask Tom and Bob and Dollie
which they liked best. That settled it. But—oh,
dear, this silence, this stiff order, this lonesome, lost
feeling that was just like a cramp about the breathing
and the voice! If grandma was here these blinds would
go up, and the sun would shine in, and the bird would
quit that dumpishness, and the cat would be playing
bo-peep around the chair with Tip, the dog, and there
would have to be a fire crackling in that stove instead
of these dead ashes. What ails everybody else? It
took grandma to keep things going. A boy might go
off down street without anything around his throat
and nobody else'd notice it. Grandma looked after a
feller. Nothing looks natural—all changed in these
few days that seem like forever."

"What's that? It's grandma's knitting. How
heavy it seems! I wonder how her poor old fingers

ever did such work; it would tire mine right away.
And, oh, to think of the hours and days and evenings
that she knitted and knitted and knitted, and it didn't
look like work, but it was! I can realize now for the
first time how all our feet stepped lightly, and we never
thought that knitting could tire anyone, it all looked
so natural, and grandma would smile at the cat rolling
and tangling the ball, and would seem so satisfied
when another pair was done; how were we to know?"

" You'd have found out if you had tried it; that's the
way with girls."

" Dick, if grandma was here she would not like to
have us disagreeing."

"Ah! perhaps these slender, shining needles and
this soft yarn that breaks so easily—who knows—
they may have wrought the difference between her
hands and those of younger ones. Of course grandma's fingers were once dainty and slender; did that
incessant knitting which grandmothers are always doing produce those enlarged joints and cramped fingers
that for years were never straight, until she was at
rest? Is it possible that we are to blame for the loss
of their grace and beauty? What a sacrifice! Which
of us would consent to become bent and crooked and
isolated, immolating self for others? Oh, we are hor-
rid! When wee Dollie sobbed, ' I don't think grandmas ought ever to die!' dear little heart, she thought
only of our loss and not of the dear one's rest. Was
there none to bring her rest but death? And we who
thought we loved her were letting burdens rest heav-

ily upon her that we would not have borne, that we would have thrown aside. O life and youth and health, how careless thou art, how blind! O wisdom, how lacking! Time, how vain thy teachings when her seventy years could not touch our careless hearts until too late! Put it away; that knitting will never be finished; the only hands that would have done it cannot, they are folded and at rest forever."

"Young Girls Don't Speak to Me."

THIS remark, uttered by a lone woman, has often recurred to me. Where we once lived we noticed almost daily a foreigner pass our house; her apparel was neat in the extreme, her hair so black and lustrous, her cheek so pale, eyes so sad, and manners so refined, I began after awhile to watch for her, for she flitted by so silently, only bowing slightly if one actually met her, I wondered who and what she was. One day I purposely met and spoke to her. She told me that her husband was an invalid, their children afar in the world, and all their possessions withheld from them on account of their receiving the gospel. Thus they had exchanged their earthly for their heavenly inheritance.

I tried to cheer her, and, thanking me, she went on her way. We moved to another locality, and a year after I met her upon a crowded street. In answer to my salutation, she looked up gravely, then smiled in recognition, and said: "You are very kind; young girls don't speak to me. I am poor, and look not fine as they do, and this seems very kind in you." Upon inquiry I learned that her husband was now dead and that she did sewing at home.

"Consider me your friend. Speak to me if I do not see you first when we meet; I often think of you." "I will. One who is so kind to the sad and lonely I cannot forget." She paused a moment, then with a quick movement drew from her neck a locket and opened it. I looked in surprise at the exquisite portrait upon ivory,—a bride adorned with jewels beside a handsome man in officer's uniform. Despite the years she had lived since then, I recognized her and realized what they had left behind them. While I thought, she turned the locket, and upon the other side looked into my eyes a child, lovely as imagination could dream. "Is she dead?" I asked. "She is living in the emperor's palace, beneath her grand uncle's guardianship, companion to a lady of rank." Her features quivered, and, hastily replacing the locket, she gave me her hand, and passed quickly on. Palace and hovel! How the thoughts rushed through my mind then and often since! Many times since I have looked for her, but we have never met since. Perhaps the poor stranger has gone where she is no longer poor or an alien.

Children, whose fathers are perhaps traveling, preaching the gospel, think how a kind salutation and

6

sympathetic interest would be valued by them, and be
kind to the new-comers you may meet. There are
many in Zion in the guise of poor and humble apparel, but I know of some such who have dwelt in
royal courts and have laid aside titles and estates to
come here and live within log houses and labor for the
necessities of life.

The King's Flower.

One early morn, from country fields,
  The market gardeners came,
With red ripe melons, "roasting ears,"
  And fruits with cheeks aflame;
And one great wagon stopped, while spoke
  The good wife at my gate;
"Will you have something, ma'am, to-day,
  They're all of them first rate?"

"I think I will; but would you like
  A handful of my flowers;
I'll gather chiefly buds; they'll bloom
  At home in a few hours."
"Oh, thank you!" Then she glanced around
  As though she something sought.
And then she knelt beside a plant
  Her earnest eye had caught.

She clasped her hands just like a child
  That finds some joyous thing,
And in her native words and smile
  Strange gladness seemed to spring;

Then, while I watched in s'lence, she
 Looked up, tears in her eyes;
"I smelled it, and the flower is here,
 Ah me; such glad surprise!"

"And do you love this flower, then,
 For it seems dear to you?
 It is the fragrant mignonette,
 And neither rare nor new."
"Yes, lady, but in mine own land
 This flower, loved by all,
 It grows in windows of the poor
 And 'round fine houses tall.

"And those who cannot buy a plant,
 And dare not ask for one,
 Can go and breathe its breath so sweet
 Out in the warm, bright sun;
 For in long beds inside the fence
 That guards the royal grounds,
 And in sweet patches o'er the lawns,
 This fair, green plant abounds.

"There, rich and poor alike may reach
 And pluck at certain hour
 These perfumed sprays; he loved them so,
 We call them 'the king's flower.'"
"Oh, gather all you wish, my friend!
 And see these small plants, too,
 That spring in plenty from the seed,
 I'll take them up for you.

"Now tell me if you know this one
 So modest, small, and blue?"

Again she smiled: "Oh, all the world
  I think knows this one, too!
I don't know what you call it here,"
  She said, as her eyes met me,
"But in mine land, so far away,
  We call it 'don't forget me.'"

I doubt if maiden fair and bright,
  And decked with love's own care,
A brighter smile of happiness
  Upon her lips could wear.
She placed them, plants and flowers, in their
  Safe place from sun or shower,
Then, as she spoke to some loved child:
  "Mine love's, mine king's own flower!"

Smile at the country teams and folk,
  But I shall ne'er forget
The lover's blue forget-me-not
  And the king's mignonette.
And when I see the wagons pass,
  There comes o'er me again
A dream of romance, royal grace,
  And she, queen of the train.

Died on the Way.

THE emigrant train had come in, and so many were
waiting, some at the depot with their own vehicles,
watching for dear ones; others hailed hacks or took
the street-cars, and a few remained, who would, as

soon as the throng cleared away a little, walk up to
the house where homeless emigrants might stay for a
few days.

A party of four by themselves attracted attention.
A man of solemn countenance, with two little children
that clung on either side of him, serious, frightened-
looking little things, although they were healthy and
neatly dressed. Beside them walked a pale woman
with a babe in her arms. Oh, those sad dark eyes!
The group, followed by a few others, moved into the
large yard, and when they entered the house, sobs and
moans and the cries of little children broke forth.
Men and women on the street had noticed and wondered, but no one liked to ask a question, and now—
well—they had gone out of sight. The man who had
charge of the house came to show them a room, and
render assistance if needed—and learned the sad story.
The baby had been ailing a little, and just before they
reached the city had died in convulsions. The parents
must go on in the morning, and the precious one be
laid among strangers. The father walked the floor in
dumb wretchedness. One after another came in with
heart-felt words. One whose heart is ever kind and
thoughtful, provided a meal for the travelers and then
went out for the little casket. His wife came in and
saw that dainty clothes were in readiness, and the husband assumed the expense of the occasion, saying it
was little enough he could do, for his own heart had
known the loss of his first child only a short time before. The tears of strangers mingled with the mourn-

ers, and it may be that the sweet sympathy helped to assuage their grief.

A young girl came in and looked on, but what was there for her to do? A sudden thought! She went out and in a few moments returned with a handful of flowers and laid them upon the casket. The poor mother took one from the rest and laid it in her pocket-book. Brief services were held, and in a few moments the little casket was carried out, the family entered a carriage, and then the few who had gathered around dispersed to their own homes. The little Saint had reached his journey's end, the Zion of his parents hopes, and now endeared to them, by that little mound, their link between earth and heaven.

In early times, before the railroad was made, many yielded to the fatigues of travel by wagon. I knew of a young girl whose lover set out for Zion, having not means sufficient for both, but intending to earn money and send back for her. It happened soon after he had gone that means came to her family, and they joyfully set forth with the next company. They had reached "the plains," and one night the young lady, after walking about awhile, sat down to rest. They had seen, day after day, newly-made graves by the wayside. "Lily, dear, perhaps that is a grave you are sitting upon; there is a board at one end." Lily rose and bent over to read the name, then cried out, "Mother!" It was the grave of the young man who had left them in England so little while before. This was Lily's first trial in coming to Zion, and the journey from that day must have been a sorrowful one.

There was an old man so poor that he was obliged to go into an institution for the poor. The officers granted him the privilege of coming out on Sunday to attend his house of worship, and knew he was a Latter-day Saint too. This was perhaps his only solace, but he kept praying that God would bring him out of that prison life and to Zion. The matter was spoken of in meeting, and word reached Salt Lake City, where an old friend of his had lately come. Very soon it was written to a friend there that the money was forwarded to pay his passage here. On Sunday he was asked after meeting if he could make ready in three days to go to Utah. He was overjoyed, and the release from the house was obtained next day. With his possessions all tied up in one red cotton handkerchief, he left the prison-like walls and went among old acquaintances, bidding them a glad good-by. It so happened that some of these found themselves able to add a few gifts and comforts for the journey, which you may be sure he appreciated. Friends related how he enjoyed the ocean trip and the cities of America, then the cars for the long, swift ride. But, alas! his feeble frame could not endure the constant excitement and change, and it was thought best to stop over a few days to give him rest. A good elder stayed with him and did all that could be done. One night the old man said, "Brother, you can go on in the morning with my body. I want it buried in Zion; but I shall be there in spirit, before you." He died happy, because he was free and on his way here.

Children who were born in Zion have no idea of the intense, prayerful longing in the hearts of those who desire to gather to God's appointed place. I know all about it, for I once lived out in the world. Can you realize the blessing of emigrating those who cannot otherwise get here? How different all would have seemed if that poor man had died away back beyond the ocean!

Children I Have Known.

Frankie.

Long ago, when I was a girl of sixteen, there was a little boy of whom I was very fond, and whom I can never forget. He was not beautiful, and his parents were not rich, but they were very comfortable. Many times have I rocked Frankie to sleep in his infancy without ever expecting that he would care any more for me than for anyone else, but, someway or other, he seemed still to cling to me when he was six and seven years old.

Frankie was rather a delicate boy in health; he could not keep up with the others in their rambles and rough play, and if he tried crossing brooks or fixing waterfalls, he always came home sopping wet; if bird'snests were the object, Frankie was almost sure to get hurt, so that at last he kept more and more at home.

How often I recall him crossing the wide clover field, then crowding through the picket fence and picking his way through the blackberry patch, at last coming down through the orchard, all in a pink perspiration, to the house. When I would meet him on the broad veranda with a soft towel to wipe his warm face, he took it so naturally, and when, after salutations, he would refresh himself with a cookie, it would not be very long before he would begin to manifest a desire for something further. "What would you like to have, Frankie?" "A red apple and a white rose, and let's us go gather bilups." I always knew what "bilups" were; they were (outside our dictionary, Frankie's and mine) violets; and they grew by the thousand in the wide meadow, under the hedges, at the tree roots, around the springs and the great watering-trough hewed out of a log; they grew everywhere, underfoot in the paths as well as in clumps of daisies, snap-dragons, lilies, scarlet lobelias, and humble buttercups.

I asked Frankie's brother, Johnnie, one day, who planted all those flowers, and Johnnie promptly answered, "My pa." But then that was his answer frequently, for he considered his pa the greatest person living, not even excepting grandma. This opinion the school-teacher also found out when he asked the small class, "Who is President of the United States?" When Abraham Lincoln's name was ready on every lip, and everybody but Johnnie knew better, he royally shouted, "My pa!"

But Frankie's the boy I was going to tell you of. With a large umbrella, a book and some cookies in a lit-

tle basket, we would start hand in hand for the meadow
and grove. When we had gathered flowers to Frankie's
satisfaction, we would go to the big trough, and there,
regularly, his face, hands and bare feet were washed
and wiped with hankerchief or apron. It was the
fashion then to wear very wide dress skirts, and I
used to sit down on the soft moss at the foot of some
tree, and Frankie would lie down on my lap, while
part of my skirt was gathered up over him to guard
off gnats, flies and other such enemies of peace and
repose. While the dear boy slept I might read, and
when he woke I would take him home to his mother.
How fondly she would smile and hasten to bring him
something nice!

One summer day Frankie wanted to go with his
brothers to some place of amusement, but his mother
gently denied him. "All the rest are going, and Dan
isn't much bigger than I am." " I know it, Frankie,
but you always get hurt when you are from home.
Won't you be willing to stay with me?" she asked,
tenderly. Before he could answer, a bird flew under
the porch, alighted upon his shoulder an instant, twit-
tered, and darted away.

" Mother, I'm going to stay close by you."

The celebration came and the boys rode away where
the drums were beating, flags flying and hurrahs now
and then rent the air.

Very dear, still dearer than ever, seemed the fragile
boy to his mother as the days went on.

One day the brothers went out for a swim in their

own little pond, not far from the house. Frankie went along just to watch them sport in the warm water. Some neighboring boys joined them soon, and Frankie went in for a short while, but the sun was too bright overhead, and he soon tired and came out. That night he was dull, and his little face was hot against his mother's cheek as he clasped her neck and bade her good-night. In the morning he was sick and the doctor ordered a bath. His delicate frame was blistered from the sun while in the pond, and he had brain fever. At intervals he was sensible. I took to him what he liked, a red apple, white rose and violets. The dear boy smiled and gathered them all around him. As he grew worse and dreaded to take his medicine, his father tried coaxing. "I'll give you this gold dollar, Frankie, if you'll take this right down." The nauseating dose was swallowed, and the hot little hand held the tiny coin awhile, then dropped it forgetfully. When the next time came for his medicine, the father held up his splendid pocket-knife as an inducement. This also won, and Frankie looked at it with a very faint smile. It was too heavy to hold. The hours wore on, and the doctor said there was hope. Try one more, that would be all. The weary sufferer looked deprecatingly at the spoon and glass and closed his eyes. There remained one thing above all others that the boy was proud of, a splendid colt owned by his father. Frankie looked into the pleading eyes of his mother and listened to his father's voice: "Frankie, if you'll take just this one dose

more I'll give you anything you ask for." The poor
little lips trembled with a glad, pitiful smile, asked
faintly, " The Black Warrior colt, pa ? " " Yes, my
boy, you shall have him," he answered, with tears of
joy in his eyes. " Bring him here." The handsome,
petted colt was led to the door, the little form was
lifted and carried to where he could put his hand upon
it. A satisfied look overspread his face and he faintly
said, " Take him back, be good to him." How happy
they all were! All the afternoon he dozed, and they
thought the rest was gathering strength. Then he
seemed to dream, for several times he called " Whoa ! "
and smiled in his sleep. Toward sundown he woke.
"Bring the Black Warrior, I'm going!" He lifted
his weak arms, and his father raised him to the fresher
air. They fell around his mother's neck; he smiled
good-by to her, and his spirit rode away.

Aggie.

Some thoughtless persons are very fond of teasing
little children, and seem to enjoy their discomfiture,
but it is an unworthy amusement. I think they little
realize how sensitive are the feelings of a child, and how
much dependence the little ones place upon words, until
they learn how untruthful grown persons can sometimes be. It is a sad thought that innocence receives
its first wrong lessons from supposed best friends.
Said a middle-aged man one day: " I never knowingly

deceive or mislead a child, or make fun of, or tease one. I speak the simple truth to them in few words. In my early childhood, one of my uncles, just to tease me, said I would have red hair when I grew older. Before this I had as good an opinion of one color of hair as another; it was the person I regarded; but the way in which he said it perplexed me, and others, seeing this, joined in the merriment, and kept it up in various ways. I became so sensitive on this subject that if anyone looked at my hair I became flushed with shame, and finally used to keep away from company as much as possible, thereby losing much enjoyment I might have shared. I had one old uncle whom I soon learned never teased or joked, and, having confidence in his perfect truthfulness, I asked him about it. His answer was a comfort to me, and I never wearied of rendering him any little attention or service I could perform; and I never see a child teased but that I just step in and take its part."

Many little children have not a wise old uncle or friend to go to, and no doubt suffer keenly sometimes. Others have sufficient spirit to defend themselves, for we are not all alike. One case comes to my mind. A dear little girl of three years used to often come across the clover-field to see me. Her name was Aggie, and she was Frankie's sister. One warm summer day she came all flushed with her little escapade, and, not seeing anyone outdoors, continued her walk along the veranda until she reached the open parlor door. The room was pretty well filled with company, and after a nasty glance across the room, Aggie started across the room to where I was sitting. As she proceeded, a person who thought to amuse himself and others by startling her, suddenly ejaculated, "Bow, wow, wow!"

Aggie turned just to see where the sound came from, and with sweet dignity answered, "Dogs belong outdoors," and then climbed up to my knee.

The laugh that followed satisfied the person that he had made a great mistake, and we all admired the little lady more than ever.

Florence.

MORE than twenty years ago, while traveling in pursuit of pleasure and information, we were stopped by heavy snows, at a town where, pleasantly for us, some families whom we had formerly known were living. There was also a friend who had visited us in our own home, during his frequent trading trips to the coast, and he urged us to make our stay with his family. They had ample accommodations for persons and animals, so we settled down for a good long visit around among old friends and new. In this family there was a sweet little girl of about eighteen months old, so fair and spiritual looking and so angelic in disposition that I soon grew very fond of her. There was little hope of her ever becoming as strong and well as the other children, for one side of her body was almost helpless.

Although the telegraph kept us informed that the roads were still unbroken, and the snow was steadily filling the great canyons ahead of us, a partial spring was dawning in the valley where we were staying. The snow melted and thinned away the icy covering of the brooks, while here a tuft of green rose by the water's edge. Now and then a bird sang, and for part of the day the sun was warm.

Early one forenoon I wrapped the dear child comfortably and told her mother I was going to give Florence the benefit of the fresh air, and would stay out as long as she seemed satisfied. The dear mother was glad, for she was too busy to do this herself. The little darling was smiles and wonder as I carried her along; she looked with such eager eyes upon the swift-running and babbling water, listening and looking into my eyes as though asking what it meant. When I gathered the few slender grasses and put them in her tiny hand she was so happy. I used to walk with her as long as she staid awake. My arms never tired of her little form, for I loved to watch her lovely eyes follow the clouds, the flight of the snow-birds, or the sway of bare branches in the frequent breeze. When walking along the thinly built-up streets, I used to sing very quietly to her, and she would finally be fast asleep.

Then I would go into the house of some acquaintance.and lay her down among the cozy quilts and pillows.

Florence always took a long nap, and when she

woke was so sweet and amiable and ready for her dinner. Then we would set out again and walk until it
was wisest to go home. Upon our return Florence
would be so cheerful that they began to build hopes.
Babies quickly learn what to expect, and before many
days had passed, she would turn around in her high-
chair and point to her hood and cloak, hung against
the wall. Often did I hasten my breakfast in answer
to those sweet eyes looking so patiently at me, and
when her mother would give her to me, all bundled
up warm, the little sweetheart would try and get one
hand out to pat our faces and hold it out for a kiss in
the little white palm. Dear child, that was little enough
to give her, just a kiss, but it satisfied her and she
would smile "good-by" as we went out.

Thanks to the spring-time, we found a few leaves
each day for Florence to hold, and a few evergreens
helped out, also a little southernwood in a south
corner gave a few sprigs to perfume the whole. Florence certainly grew better; she even tried one day to
stand by a chair, but it was almost too soon. Sometimes a trinket from my trunk found its way into her
lap, and her pleasure seemed so gentle and complete.

The time drew near for us to resume our journey,
and when I looked at the delicate child that still
needed her daily walk, my heart reproached me for
going away. I felt followed by the thought of a sweet
little pale face waiting for me, and a word of permission
when the others were starting would have held me
back with the child I had grown to love so. But I

7

was to go on, and when I clasped her frail form in my
arms, then gave her to her mother, it would have been
hard for me to express the thoughts that arose. It
looked selfish in me to go, when perhaps I *might* have
been the means of saving her life by staying.

After we reached "the city" and the months rolled
by until October, and the conference folks filled the
streets, who should call one day but the parents of
Florence! She was not with them, and I dared not to
ask, but they understood. "Florence died in the
summer. She missed those walks, and she never
grew stronger but just faded away." Sometimes
memory brings before me a fair little face, lighted by
blue, wishful eyes, and outlined by flossy golden
tresses, with outreached hands that ask me to take
her, but when I whisper "Florence," it is gone.

Little Lizzie.

SHALL I tell you of another dear child I once knew?
She was named for a friend, and to distinguish them,
for they lived in the same house, they called her
"Little Lizzie." Her face was a winsome little picture;
she had a way of holding her head on one side, in a
shy, modest fashion, that was like no one else. Lizzie's
hair was a golden brown and so soft and light, like
silk floss, that part of it was afloat around her head
most of the time, for a breath of wind through the

LITTLE LIZZIE.

window, or even her own restless movements, kept it
in a stir.   Such glowing red cheeks, such dark blue
eyes, almost black, and such long lashes are seldom
seen.   Little Lizzie was such a mite to begin with that
when a year old babies half her age were larger.   She
was just like a bird bobbing around and twittering her
sweet little tunes, for Lizzie was always singing to
herself when only two years old.   Her very serious-
ness would make one smile; those lovely eyes were
so large and bright, so wide open, "they were just
more than one person's share of beauty," someone
said.

Lizzie's father had many very choice flowers in his
garden and many arranged on stands also.   Sometimes she tried to rearrange these, but always to the injury of her clothing and sometimes the destruction of
pots and flowers.   How innocently she would survey
the disaster, and, patiently clasping her hands, whisper
a petition for forgiveness.   Somehow, a gentle chiding,
but nothing severer, followed when these things happened.   The transplanting was also closely observed
by her, and the good old gardener had no idea what
was to follow.   One warm afternoon her sister and I
spread a rug upon the bedroom floor, closed the door
and windows, arranged our pillows, and prepared for
a cool time of reading or napping.

I awoke with a gentle breath fanning my face, and
just opening my eyes met close to me those of little
Lizzie, wonder-wide, gazing upon me.   Garden soil
was upon her vivid cheeks, and about the corners of

her pretty lips, and those clean Saturday afternoon clothes—what would her mother say?

"Little Lizzie, what have you been doing?"

"Been a-digging the flowers out of the ground," said she sweetly, and, changing from all fours to an upright position, we saw upon the carpet the devastation she had wrought, the wilted plants. I roused her sister, and we went out. "Let's get them back in the ground as quick as we can," said Mary; and we worked quick, I can tell you! "If you were just more than two years old. I know what I'd do," said Mary, pressing the dirt around the last plant.

Little Lizzie answered with a sudden hug and kiss. She had a habit of going outdoors nearly every afternoon and returning in a very quiet mood. Once, as I saw her going, trailing her pretty sunbonnet along by the strings, I asked her, "Where are you going, Little Lizzie?" She paused, looked back, and answered seriously, "I'm going to seek my heavenly Father." "Where are you going to seek him?" "In the barn," she replied and went out. The dear old grandmother followed soon after (no one else went), and when she returned she said: "We ain't as near to God as that blessed child is; I've been listening to her." "What was she saying?" tremulously asked Mary. "Forgive me 'nother time, Lord Jesus," and I came away. We were all silent awhile and had our own thoughts.

The piety of this dear child remained a feature of her after years. She was gifted in music, and her parents would often listen with strange feelings to the harmonies that her own spirit called forth from the keys, with snatches of words here and there just as they came to her. "She sings, and her soul is her teacher," said her father. When she was twelve years old, her sister six years older died. From that time Lizzie was silent and lonely. One day they missed her, and after searching vainly her father went to the sister's grave to weep over the sorrow that he felt was drawing around them. A little slender figure lay across the grave; it was Lizzie. They talked together, and he found out how she was missing her mate. Often after this they found her there, and they knew she was longing to go to her absent sister, and it was not long before her health yielded to her sorrow. When the end was near and she heeded not those around her, she repeated again so sweetly her own little prayer: "Lord Jesus, forgive my sins once more and take me."

Her sins! a gentle girl of thirteen. What had she to fear? Might we all be as well prepared.

No doubt the loving sisters were reunited to walk together in happiness, awaiting the coming of parents and kindred.

Lost in the Canyon.

Two little girls, neatly dressed as they should be for a pleasant walk, and pretty lunch-baskets filled with the nicest of things, started out for a walk up the canyon. There was a good road for a long distance, then it branched off right and left, the trees grew taller, the bushes thicker and more tangled, and they felt as if they were away off in a little world of their own. How nice it was! Birds came close overhead, and they saw several live chipmunks.

After gathering a great many flowers and eating lunch, and having had enough walking for awhile, they began telling certain fairy stories in which the parties all lived out in the woods; they also discussed "Robinson Crusoe" and the "Swiss Family Robinson," finally agreeing that an outdoor life was the best and nicest, and that gypsies had a fine time traveling and seeing the sights of the

LOST IN A CANYON.

world—no house-work, no crowding of neighbors, all
free and easy.

The day wore along until afternoon, when the
canyon began to grow dark very fast. All at once a
thought struck Addie—"bears!" Gracie immediately
remembered and related to her shuddering companion a horrible encounter that took place in "some
canyon, may be this one," between a bear and a man.
It was also remembered that some bears can travel as
fast as a horse can run. In the remembered event
nothing was left by the rapacious animal to identify
the missing man excepting a tin dinner pail, which
must have been overlooked by the bear, and which
was recognized by relatives, by a place that had been
soldered, also another place with a blue and white
gingham string drawn through a hole. "For truth?"
asked Addie. "That's just the way I remember hearing it told," replied Gracie, evasively. "Do you think
we'd better start home?" asked Addie indifferently
(that is, as indifferently as she could speak under the
circumstances). "I guess it's early yet, but if you
wish we might walk slowly down a little way," said
Gracie. With a show of some reluctance, Addie
gathered her treasures together, and they started at a
sauntering gait, which somehow was gradually acceler-
ated without the apparent notice of either, at least it
was not objected to as tiring.

These children had gone farther up the canyon than
they had realized; the many charms had beguiled
them along, their light and healthy forms feeling no

fatigue for a long while. Suddenly, a low rumble was heard that increased and seemed to be rapidly coming in their direction.

"Oh, dear! Gracie, did you ever hear that canyons are awful places for storms?" "Yes, Addie, and for swollen streams, and cloud-bursts," replied Gracie. "It's raining! Are there any caves?" "Only way up on the side, down yonder." "Let's take hold of hands and run!" "We'd have to drop our flowers." "I don't care. Hurry!"

Away they went, the wind driving the rain right in their faces; the pretty hats with daisy wreaths were dripping; the pretty light print dresses hung straight down, and their shoes were sopping wet.

"Do you think our folks will come after us when they know it's storming up here?"

Addie began to cry, and Gracie, instead of being able to console her, exclaimed: "We've come a long ways now and I believe we're lost!" Looking around and not being able to see very far through the rain, Addie replied: "I believe so too. What shall we do?"

Now these were both very good children and had been rightly raised, but in their hurry and flight had forgotten what that morning they would not have thought they could forget, and that was to remember how the heavenly Father is watching over us all and is able and willing to protect us. But, standing there in dismay, it came to them.

"Let's pray that we may get home!" "Oh, yes!"

Then they knelt down in the mud, with the wind

and rain roaring around them and the creek foaming
and raging below, and asked God to please show them
the way home, never doubting that He would hear
them through all the storm.

As they rose from their knees, Addie said: "Now
let's turn round and round, and when we stop, start
right off in that direction." Just as they had begun
to turn "round and round," a sound as of some large
animal running towards them came nearer and nearer.
They stopped, hand in hand, and waited its coming.
How big it looked through the rain!

"Hallo! Who's here? How's this?" Explana-
tions followed, and the man, who had started out to
hunt a stray horse, changed his mind. He drew them
up, one behind and the other before him, and went
down the road as fast as he could. At one of the first
houses (it was his own) he called and someone came
out. "Take these children in and put dry things on
them." It seems that fortunately he had little girls
about the same age, and they were soon redressed and
supplied with suitable refreshment to counteract the
effects of the wetting. The storm cleared away before long, and while two anxious mothers were watching at their gates, they saw two little girls (but not
dressed like theirs), with each a bundle, approaching.

Their story was soon told, and, oh, how thankful
were those mothers to the solitary horseman who had
brought their dear ones through three miles of storm
and fear, and how proud too, and grateful that their
children remembered to pray! "It was in answer to

our prayers that the man came to our relief," said Addie. "And how quick He answered us!" added Gracie. "Children, God always goes part way to his creatures. He knew your peril and sent his messenger. Remember always in your troubles, God is on the way to help you, and you have only to let your heart go out to receive him and he is there;" and this lesson was ended with four kisses.

You may think this story to be imaginary, but Gracie and Addie are now young ladies, and still live in Salt Lake City. Their own happy mothers told it all to me.

Adela and Minnie.

AMONG the playmates of my childhood was an Indian girl about twelve years of age. After the Latter-day Saints had left our town, and we could not yet go with them, there were few Mormon children remaining, and our parents did not care to mingle with those who despised our people and our faith. Upon our farm, as was the custom in Southern California, several Indians were employed, and Adela was a daughter of one of the women who did washing and sewing for the white people. Adela's great grandfather and uncle also lived upon our farm, at a convenient distance from the house. Adela went to school with us when she wished, and learned all our songs, also how to crochet lace and make doll clothing. Adela could skip rope the longest, swing the highest, play ball the best, and taught us very pretty games of playing ball. One was like this: As many as chose could form a circle, standing a rod or so apart, and throw the ball to the next. As the circle was very large if the number of girls was seven or eight, and each girl had a ball to throw with one hand and catch another from the next playmate, you can see how pretty it would look, a perfect string of balls flying around the circle all the time. It required a watchful eye and skillful hands to keep the game going without a break, and it was the stillest game of ball I ever knew, while in progress; but if a catcher missed, it was noisy enough till we got started again.

Then Adela could roll hoop the prettiest, always coming out ahead at the end of the lane; climb the highest for a peep into a bird's nest, and dive into deep water where we were almost afraid to look at her. In our bow and arrow practice she could strike the mark oftener than we could, and would send her arrows one after the other like shooting stars, till her quiver was empty

How many a day of innocent and healthful games and pleasures we had together. I do not remember that we ever had a misunderstanding in all our days together.

Adela would come early in the morning and sometimes stay till after prayer-time. If I had work or sewing to do first, she helped me. Always gentle and obliging, never rude or obtrusive, Adela was a pattern to many white girls. When her people went into the mountains, and brought back nice things, Adela always brought us some, as though we were one of the family. Adela was very pretty, and her voice was as sweet as one ever heard.

We used to coax her to sing Indian songs to us and then tell us their meaning. When Adela was older, she went with her friends on a picnic in the mountains, and while away took sick and died. I sorrowed long after my gentle mate, and can never forget her tender face, graceful form and sweet voice. As Latter-day Saints, we have a knowledge of the history of the Indian races, and look forward to their occupying a more exalted condition. How happy a time that will be, for many of them are worthy, their hearts as loving and sometimes more faithful than ours.

Let me tell you about Minnie, an Indian babe. Her mother was a relative of Adela's, perhaps a cousin. The parents of Minnie worked on our farm for seven years. Lisifa, the mother, was of the Cabezon tribe, of California, and Pete, the father, was from the Muddy River tribe, in Nevada.

Once, when I was away from home, my mother wrote that Lisifa had a little girl, and desired me to send it a name. I was in Salt Lake City, and replied that I would soon start home, but if the name suited them, call her Minnie.

You see I thought that would be easy for them to speak and remember. Well, on my return I found she was a dear little thing, and soon took great inter-

est in her. Her parents had moved into an adobe
storehouse of ours, and her mother was a good housekeeper and seamstress and kept her baby more comfortably clothed than many richer babies I know of.
Every morning before breakfast Minnie was ready
in clean, fresh clothing for anyone to take her, and
soon learned to watch for me and hold out her pretty
hands. By regular bathing in water in which some
fragrant herb had been steeped, Minnie's complexion
was much fairer than might have been expected.
Her hair shone like black satin, and her eyes were
soft and black like a deer's. She used to sit on my
lap while I sewed on the machine, and was very cautious not to touch anything, but would watch the
movements with great interest. Minnie liked the
movement of the treadle and would kick vigorously
during a pause for the treadle to "get up" again. She
often fell asleep, her head resting on her dimpled arms
crossed on the machine table.

Then I would lay her on the sofa, and cover her
with shawl and mosquito-bar. If her mother happened
to wonder about her baby, and looked into the room,
she would smile and go back to her work. We were
all fond of her. As she grew older, when father came
home from the office at night, Minnie was always on
the lookout, and her little shiny black head could be
seen bobbing along the drive, just showing above the
fleur-de-lis that bordered each side.

Pete was the driver, and father had told him to be
watchful or he might sometime drive against her; for

the carriage-way was in curves instead of a straight avenue. Pete would jump down and lift her up beside him, and they were very happy. "Not like other poor Indian babies," he would say appreciatively. Pete wanted Minnie to go to school when old enough, and my parents promised him that it should be so. However, when Minnie was eighteen months old, the way opened for part of our family to come to Utah.

Mr. Lord, a good man, promised to do as well by Pete and his family as we had, so there was a good prospect for them. They wanted to take our little hand-cart, that was used for fruit.gathering, and come with us. "I could haul Minnie and our clothes, and Lisifa and I could walk," he said; but it was explained to him how we would not have a fine property in Utah, and an income to pay them wages, and that they had best remain with Mr. Lord until we could send for them. Little Minnie was asleep when we came away. Father had to stay behind awhile to collect money not then due.

One night someone rapped at his bedroom door. He asked who was there, and the answer was, "Pete."

Father arose, and, asking him in, saw that he could hardly speak, for trouble. "What is it, Pete, tell me, poor boy."

"Minnie is dead. They had fly-paper and she put some in her mouth. Mrs. Lord could not save her. Write to the folks." Father tried to console him. "Thank you, Colonel; I guess I go back to her mother." And he went alone, his lonely, sad, three-

miles' walk. We wrote to them. Father read the
letter aloud and gave it to Pete. They pressed it to
their cheeks, put it carefully away, and went home.
That was twenty-one years ago. Just lately I heard
from them. Pete had been asking an old friend if she
knew anything of us. When I answered the lady's
letter, I sent my picture, and she showed it to them.
"Most 'ike her mother. Tell her about my boy I've
got." I have written to him that a better day for
his people is near at hand, and that he too may yet
through knowledge perform a part.

Johnny Layton Kills a Bear.

ONCE when traveling, we were "snowed in," and as
there were prospects of bad roads for weeks yet, we
rented a room in a nice little rock house, in which
lived a small family. Of the three children, Johnny,
who was next to the baby, was a robust little fellow
three years old, and he was such a chatter-box that we
found great entertainment in listening to him, and always found him truthful, too, which is a rare quality
in "story-telling."

Johnny used to come in to see us very early in the
morning, and we were fond of having him take breakfast with us, it was such a novelty to watch his ener-
getic way of speaking and gesticulating.

Sometimes his mother hastened after him, fearing that

we were becoming annoyed, but it was not so. One morning, after another heavy snowfall, a tap was heard, and, opening the door, there stood Johnny, in great haste to tell us something. "Well, Johnny, sit down with us to breakfast, and tell us while we eat."

Johnny climbed upon the pillow which sister placed on the chair for his benefit, and began, " I killed a bear!" "You didn't do anything of the kind!" said sister, but Johnny looked as dead in earnest as a boy could look, and answered quietly and firmly, "I did."

"Tell us all about it," said ma, who always believed in giving children a chance. "Was it a toy bear?" I asked. "No, it wasn't; it was a true bear, as big as a —big calf, and you ought to have heard it roar! My!" And Johnny stood up on the round of the chair and held up his arms. "You'd better sit down ; you'll lose your balance," said sister. Johnny sat down and proceeded to fill his cheeks with a piece of pie. His eyes roamed from one to the other, and when he had managed to swallow the greater portion, so that breathing became less difficult, he was going to resume, but his mother knocked and came in. "O Johnny, what makes you do like this? I'm ashamed of you!" "Never mind, he's welcome, and he was just going to tell us something very wonderful," said ma. "That bear I killed—" he began. "Johnny Layton," interrupted his mother, "what do you mean by talking like that?" "I ain't talking like that; that bear I killed—" "Oh, you little story-teller! sticking

8

to it when you know we all know better. You never saw a bear; you don't know what they're like." "I do! I've seen their pictures, lots of 'em." The laugh which followed this speech did not disconcert Johnny; he had proved that he knew what a bear looked like, and it would be easy enough to prove the rest. Ma looked kindly at Johnny, and he resumed: "That bear I killed—" "Johnny, don't tell any more, or I'll have to whip you for story-telling; it's time to quit now."

"I think we had better hear the story. I think it will come out all right," said ma, and Johnny began again and rushed right through. "That bear I killed was up in Pine Valley, where I went with my pa to get a load of wood. [The auditors glanced at each other.] My pa had gone for the horses to bring home the wood, and that bear came right out behind a tree and jumped at our wagon, and when I hollered at him he stopped!" Johnny took no discouragement from his mother's mortified expression, my amazement, nor sister's look, which said plainly enough, "You little fibber!" but went on: "Then he *come!* a-jumping, and I climbed on the load, and jumped on him and killed him!" There was no mistaking his earnestness; he fairly glowed with excitement. "He's going to be sick with brain fever," said the mother tremulously.

"Was it after you had the molasses candy, Johnny?" inquired ma. "Yes, I went off and left my candy, and I want it now," and Johnny began to slide down, and was soon out of the room. "It was all a dream! I

wouldn't scold him; he believes it every bit." "O
Sister J., perhaps he did dream that; he awoke with a
scream, and, as soon as he dressed, he ran in here,"
said Johnny's mother, smiling in relief. By this time
he was back with his candy, and no one made any
further effort to induce him to retract his statement.
Johnny appeared satisfied at having finished the narra-
tive, and at our having been unable to deprive him of
the honor of the occasion.

When Johnny grew older, of course he was able to
understand the wide difference between dreams and
realities.

Hired Himself Out for Ten Cents.

I KNOW a dear boy and have known him from the
time he was a lovely babe in the arms of his lady
mother.

Many of our valued friends who were reared in most
comfortable circumstances, left all for the Gospel's
sake, and in their homes here in Zion have been far
differently situated as to incomes and conveniences.
It was the case with this family.

There was a sweet little sister about three months
old, the delight of the house. She was often restless
with pain, and this distressed my hero, who was about
seven years of age, and he was very anxious to know
of something that would do her good. A lady who
was making a call said, " If the baby had some pepper-

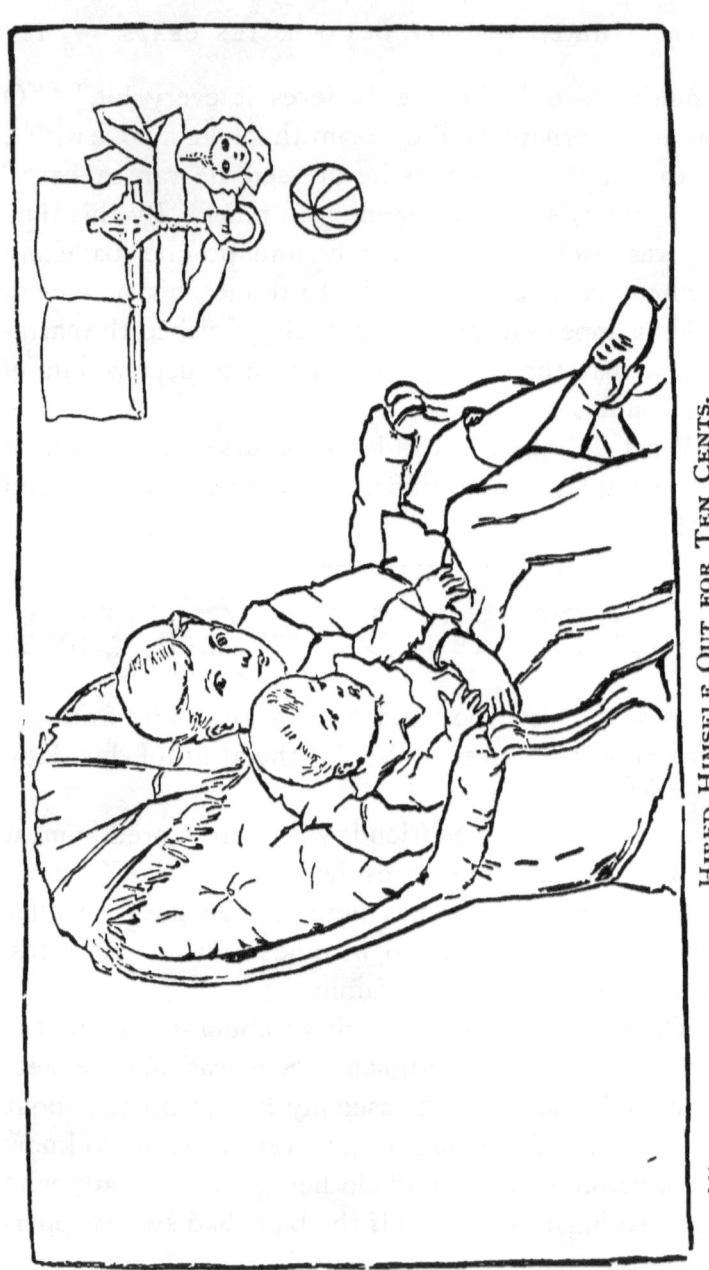

HIRED HIMSELF OUT FOR TEN CENTS.

mint, it would cure all that." The boy slipped quietly out of the room, and was seen no more that day until sundown, when he entered the house with a bright smile and had a little paper bag in his hand.

"My dear son, where have you been? I have looked for you and called and did not know what to do." "Mother, I heard what Mrs. Clark said this morning and went out to hunt work. I offered myself to Mrs. Brown, the boarding-house keeper, for ten cents for the day, and here are three sticks of peppermint candy for the baby." After a happy embrace of the little sister, he triumphantly placed one stick within her hand. You may be sure his mother gave him a fond kiss and was proud to have a boy like that, who would go out with the spirit of a man and find a way to earn what he wanted, and all by the whisper of love.

The Canary and the Prophecy.

THERE was another boy, a little older. He was very fond of birds and felt willing to do anything he was able to perform, to earn money enough to buy himself a canary and a cage. Very soon he managed to find employment, sometimes one thing and sometimes another, always so prompt, faithful and cheerful that he soon found persons inquiring after him, instead of having to hunt work.

After what seemed a very long time, for birds used to be very dear in those days, my little friend had a sum

THE CANARY AND THE PROPHECY.

sufficient, and started out, as happy as could be, to make his purchase. The bird was selected; the price was $5.00, and the cage was $1.50. He then bought ten cents' worth of seed to feed it, intending to soon purchase more. The merchant began laughing and ridiculing him about the small package of feed. The poor boy left the store with his treasure, but far from being as happy as when he entered it, and going home with burning cheeks and heavy heart, he told his gentle mother.

The father arrived and was informed and immediately started down town. When he entered the store, the merchant knew something was coming, and soon found out what it was. "Where was your manhood when you could ridicule a little child that had worked for weeks and weeks to pay you a high price for a bird and cage? I promise you here that that boy will rise and have name and wealth when you are down and poor! You may watch him and I will watch you!"

The man of avarice shrank before the eye and voice of the man who uttered those significant words.

Within ten years the merchant had lost his fine store, his comfortable home property, and was scarcely earning a living, besides being an object of sympathy, from his altered health and dejected appearance. Two years later, and while he still lived, the boy had realized the fulfillment of that portion of his father's prophecy which related to him, by an office of trust and emolument, which his proven integrity and ability had qualified him for, being conferred upon him.

In Far-Away Bohemia.

NOT many months ago something was shown and told to me of a youth whom I had known in his infancy. Time flies swiftly, and I could hardly realize that the lovely boy I had once held in my arms was already a man and a hero.

I was visiting a lady when another entered the room with something carefully folded in her hands, and said, "I am going to show you this, because you will appreciate it and understand my feelings." What do you think it was? A dark blue apron, made to come up across the breast and down below the knees, like a butcher's apron. Then she told me its story. Her son had been called to go and preach the gospel in Bohemia. He was very young, and must have been filled with the spirit of his mission to go cheerfully so far away across the world among a strange people, he who had never before been separated from his own kindred and mountain home.

The country to which he went was a marked spot upon the earth for the great scenes which had been enacted there, and must be dear to the Lord for the sake of the great and good men who laid down their lives for love of his word.

More than a thousand years ago, many of that people were searching for the truth with such earnestness that they cheerfully devoted their fortunes and their lives to that end. They lived one long-continued war-

fare in its pursuit, and many at last perished in the
flames or by the sword, but Bohemia was the place to
which still came the lovers of the Bible to speak together in secret, and from there the truth spread into
other countries, while the faithful at home hid and
preserved the Holy Bible from complete destruction,
through century after century. Nation after nation
made war upon these religionists, and they were deprived of their rights one by one, until neither their
property nor lives were safe.

So to that country stained with the blood, her
streams clouded with the ashes, of martyrs, went Louis,
to tell them a new meaning of the Scriptures, tidings
of great joy, the restoration of the Gospel, and the
second coming of our Lord and Saviour to reign upon
the earth, surrounded by the pure, the noble, and all
who have suffered and died for his cause.

But the laws of that country are still very strict,
and Louis was compelled to adopt a disguise by which
he could enter the houses and leave a few printed
pages to open the minds of the people to further inquiry. So he, with a companion, traveled together as
tinkers, with an outfit for mending kitchen utensils,
and this was the apron he wore.

Oh, what humility! thus to descend to fulfill the
mission of the Lord Jesus Christ.

Can you imagine the anxiety, the hopes and prayers, of his father, his loving mother, and all the kindred
who had known him from infancy to manhood, while
he wandered through that land whose record was vol-

ume after volume of religious discussions and perse-
cutions ?

But he who called him to go, brought him back in
safety and honor. Joy and peace are theirs for faith
that has been proven, and work well done. There
are many nations yet to be visited and invited to the
truth, and the missionary can truly see that " the har-
vest is great but the laborers are few," and the hearts
of men are inclined more to seeking after riches and
pleasure than giving their service unto the Lord.

All honor to the young missionary who wore the
garb of humility and bore his Master's message.
Such are builders in His kingdom, and He will delight
to own and bless them.

Abraham.

BEFORE the death of Pres. Brigham Young, there
lived in Utah an orphan youth named Abraham.   His
opportunities for education had been limited, but he
strove to learn all he could by observation, and listened
to the conversations of those whom he knew to be wiser
than himself.   He was industrious and rigidly ab-
stained from the use of tea, coffee, tobacco and spirit-
uous drinks, believing them to be injurious to the
system.

It was a rule with him to consider before speaking,
and to avoid all contentions, consequently his name

was never associated with any quarrel or provocative speech, and, although his acquaintances could never draw him into any mischievous raids or pranks, they always had a good word for him. Before he was nineteen, he had made two trips to California and back with freighters, and one to Nevada. At the latter place he was offered good wages by a dairyman, and accepted the situation. With his first money he obtained from Salt Lake City a set of church-books and one year's subscription to the Deseret *News*, wishing to inform himself upon his religion and keep up with events as they transpired among our people, so as not to appear as a stranger when he should return. Abraham never read trifling books or papers, his little leisure was too precious. He was the only Mormon on the ranch, and they began teasing him, but he treated them with such quiet dignity that they soon changed their course, and if they asked any questions they were respectful ones, which he answered to the best of his ability. At the end of the first year he sent his money with a letter to Pres. George Q. Cannon, asking him to invest it for him in what he considered the best way. That gracious and kind-hearted gentleman accepted the responsibility and purchased shares in Zion's Co-operative Mercantile Institution, and sent certificates of the same to his young acquaintance.

For Abraham's second year's labor he received, beside some money, two fine mares with colts, beside them a new wagon and harness. "That means travel," thought he, and told his employer, who, with all his men, now liked the steady youth so well that he offered increase of wages if he would stay. "I'm going home," said Abraham, smiling. Highwaymen were common in that region. The Indians also were troublesome sometimes. When Abraham expressed his intention of going the old, unfrequented road, fears were declared, but he smiled as he bade them good-by. One day he observed Indians following him, and when at night they came to his camp, he treated them kindly, sharing his supper with them, and then preached to them upon the history of their ancestors, as learned from the Book of Mormon. They traveled with him three days and nights. Next day, as he was descending an old dugway, his team was blockaded by a deep snow-drift. With his ax he cleared the way for several rods, then went on without further trouble. Arriving in Salt Lake City in August, 1871, he repaired to the office of Pres. Brigham Young, where he found Pres. George Q. Cannon, and reported himself. That gentleman was so pleased he led him into an inner room and said: "President Young, I would like you to hear this young brother's experience." Abraham answered many questions, all of which proved him to be no idle student of theology or current events. "Well, Brother Abraham, what are you going to do next?" "I have no plans of my own, sir. I was going to ask counsel." "Are you willing to go on a mission?" "Yes, sir." "Would you prefer going to your kindred in New Hampshire or assist in colonizing Arizona?" "Your choice, President Young, will be my preference." Our leader reflected a moment. "What does your property amount to? and what is it?" Abraham made the statement. "Brother Abraham, are you willing to take counsel if I ask you to go on a mission and give your property into the United Order?" "Yes, sir."

"That's the right spirit," said he reflectively. Abraham arose to go. "Where shall I deliver my team, President Young?" "Are you quite sure you are willing, Brother Abraham?"

"Yes, sir," said he, smiling. "I want to be of use in this church, and any way that is acceptable to it is acceptable to me." President Young arose, took the young man by the hand, and said solemnly: "Brother Abraham, take your team where it suits you best; you are the most proper person I know to possess it. I give you a mission to find a good wife and make you a home wherever you wish in this Territory. If you choose to remain here, employment will be given you. I wish we had more men like you, and I say, God bless you!"

Such was the spirit and counsel of the man whom many judge unjustly; such was ever his fatherly spirit to the faithful.

His counsel was followed, and the hero of my story still lives and holds the confidence and esteem of all good men wherever he goes. When his boys and girls read this, I hope it will give them as much pride and pleasure as it has given me in recording it.

Dialogue between a Christian and Infidel.

(*Enter book agent.*) "Good-day, madame, I would like to show you an interesting work?"

"What is it, sir?"

"A work showing the errors of the Bible, as arranged carefully by our most advanced scientists and free-thinkers."

"Sir, I have no use for such a work; the Bible is the book for me."

"Madame, I can show you that the Bible is of no use in this age of progress. You cannot show me any benefit to humanity in the whole volume of errors and inconsistencies."

"Sir, I can take one sentence and prove to you that it contains a commandment to all the human race, a rule that would benefit the whole earth."

(*Agent, sneering*) "I'd like to know what it is."

"'Thou shalt love the Lord thy God with all thy heart and thy neighbor as thyself.' If you refuse the first part as a commandment to yourself, the last five words are enough to guide the whole world to dwell in order and harmony. If these words were lived up to, there would be no wrong done by one to another, consequently no crime or sorrow."

"That's all right, that's Bob Ingersoll's doctrine."

"Sir, I would not set Bob Ingersoll before his Creator, nor give him the credit of that command; if he uses it he is only a plagiarist; God is the author of those words."

"Never mind, what use is your Bible anyway? The Christians are a small part of the world; millions get along without it.

"Yes, the heathen; who would wish to dwell among them?"

"Oh, I'd just as soon live among them as with the Christians!"

"Well, sir, I think that would be the proper place for all infidels to go to; they would soon be exterminated."

"I guess I'll stay among civilization; and I'll ask you to show, madame, any noted infidel that was ever guilty of crime."

"Sir, infidelity is the greatest of all crimes—to deny your Creator."

"I don't acknowledge any creator."

"Who sent you here upon earth?"

"Oh, I just happened here by process of evolution!"

"Indeed! A Darwin theory. Well, I'd rather claim descent from a heavenly Parent than from a monkey."

"Well, madame, I don't believe in a God anyway."

"Neither did Saul, until he was struck by lightning, but he found out the truth then."

"I don't know about that; we have no proof of such statement; why, madame, the New Testament was not written till three hundred years after the death of Christ, and then all those things might have been exaggerated."

" Sir, the apostles did not live to be three hundred
years old, and Josephus, a Jewish historian of undis-
puted authority, confirmed the existence, the wondrous teachings, of our Saviour, his death, and the
labors of the apostles also. Behold the destruction of
Jerusalem and the scattering of the Jews in fulfillment
of our Lord's prophecies !   History confirms it all."

" Well, madame, many of your Christians have deserted their own principles, but even Voltaire never
recanted, nor any other infidel."

"The French people suffered revolutions and massa-
cres for many years as a penalty for receiving the
writings of Voltaire ; and Tom Payne, a great infidel,
did repent on his death-bed all he had written."

" That is a ministerial fabrication. Free-thinkers
don't believe it."

"We Christians have as good a right to believe he
did recant as you infidels to say he did not."

"Yes, but when I die, if you should witness my
death you would see me pass away an infidel still."

"I would not wish to witness your passing away;
I would rather attend the death-bed of a good Christian, at peace with all mankind and his Creator, and
mourned by his fellow-creature."

" Well, when I die I'll just turn up my toes and go
off regardless of everything."

"I don't know whether you'll turn up your toes
according to your own plan or not. You may be
destroyed suddenly by flood, explosion, or some other
unexpected calamity, and where do you expect to go
after you die?"

"Nowhere; that's the end of me."

"Sir, I think you will find that you will have to go somewhere and meet an account of yourself."

"Well, madame, I'd advise you to read your Bible."

"I have read it more than any other book, in fact I learned my letters on my grandfather's knee, from the great family Bible; it was my primer, reader, story-book and history all in one."

"I guess I'll be going!   I see you keep bees?"

"Yes.   Do you think they are infidels or Christians?"

"Infidels."

"No, sir! they are Christians.   They keep the laws that their Creator made for them.   'God made man upright, but he hath sought out many inventions.' Infidelity is one of them.   These Christian bees are contented, industrious, and orderly.   Infidels are uneasy, live a life of fault-finding, and die unsatisfied and miserable, after all their endeavors."

"I am prepared, madam, to resist scientifically all the arguments of Christianity against infidelity.   I am immovable!   No matter what may be brought."

(A bee stings him and he fights back and beats a retreat.)

"Bravo! for the insect defender of the faith.   Mr. Infidel, I thought you were immovable!"   (*Exit* infidel.)

9

The Power of Prayer.

We have the promise of the heavenly Father that "the prayer of faith shall save the sick."

Where children are taught this from infancy, they are more sure to have faith than are those who are converted to religion later in life. An incident came to my hearing lately which I will relate.

A member of our ward is absent on a mission in Norway. After many months of travel and preaching, he became sick with a fever, and was taken to a hospital instead of to his friends. He sent a cablegram to his family informing them of his extreme sickness. This gave the hospital authorities knowledge of his being a Mormon, and they carried him out of the building and left him in the street. It took the sick man five hours to crawl half a mile to the house of a friend, where he was kindly cared for, but he rapidly grew worse from the effects of the harsh treatment and exposure he had endured.

When the cable message reached his family in Utah, they gathered together in solemn prayer in behalf of the sick husband and father.

The mother was a member of a Primary Association, and when the meeting was held, they made the far-off missionary the subject of prayer, all repeating in unison the words of the speaker. In due time a letter came stating that on a certain afternoon he began to recover, and next day resumed his travel on foot and preaching.

Upon comparing dates it was proven that his restoration began upon the very day of their united petitions in his behalf.

The ministering angels, with healing and blessing, had sped swifter than the winds, and God had fulfilled his promise to the prayer of faith of the little ones at home.

The Pirate and the Doves.

At anchor near a lonely isle
    The pirate's vessel lay.
The call and song of many a bird
    Rang near and far away,
And luscious fruits and cooling shade
    Beguiled their resting-day.

Idly they strayed, or lounged around,
    Safe from the burning sun,
Or filled the dusty water kegs,
    Or brought down, one by one,
From leafy heights, for plumage bright,
    The spoil of bow and gun.

They drew from out the brooklet clear
    The trout at fearless play,
And pillaged from the isle's gray rocks
    The honey stored away
By busy bees, and gathered fruits
    With none to say them nay.

Would you not think these men had cause
  To bend the grateful knee
When God had placed there, fresh to hand,
  Such blessings bounteously,
And caves for shelter when it stormed
  Upon the restless sea?

But no, these men cared not for Him
  Who made earth, sea, and sky,
Nor cared for fellow-creatures' rights
  Or helpless beings' cry;
They pillaged earth and sea alike
  And lived but to defy.

They only waited for the night
  To sail from shelt'ring shore,
For as they watched, a noble ship
  That precious cargo bore,
Passed gently by, and loud they laughed
  Above the ocean's roar.

The pirate's ship, like bird on wing,
  Sped with the sun or gale;
Her lightness and her proven strength
  Had ne'er been known to fail,
And so, secure for stealthy chase,
  They watched the flitting sail.

And, lounging, one apart half dreamed,
  When a soft murmur broke
The sense of sleep—and with a start
  The bearded man awoke;
It seemed as though somewhere afar
  To him a sweet voice spoke.

He listened, and it all was clear,
   Again it called above,
And mem'ry brought forgotten scenes
   Of home, and youth, and love,
It was the same his mother fed—
   A gentle, cooing dove.

Again he leaned beside her knee
   And watched her tender hand
Strew grain and crumbs, and saw the birds
   In fearless, pretty band,
Gather around her garments' hem,
   And close where he did stand.

Then he remembered how she led
   His steps through paths of light,
How every day's account was sealed
   With her fond kiss at night,
And how her prayers had been that God
   Would guide him in the right.

Her parting kiss, the promise asked—
   "Will you remember, love,
To choose the right and shun the wrong,
   And trust to Him above,
When dangers press, to bring you home,
   My heart's dear, soul-white dove?"

How many years had passed, and he,
   Soul-stained, with hand upraised
'Gainst all her life had taught was good,
   Beheld himself, amazed;
And back o'er broken wrecks of years
   His spirit sadly gazed.

And still the little dove cooed on,
  And others flocking came.
The pictures grew like life—almost
  He heard her speak his name,
Its cadence just for him alone,
  It was the very same.

And those white doves, with fearless wings,
  Around and near him flew,
They almost seemed like messengers ;
  Their bright eyes looked him through
And seemed to say, ''She sent us forth
  Who waits at home for you.''

And all the while the restless flock
  Seemed evermore to coo—
He could make out no other words
  But ''waits for you! for you!''
They pierced his ears, rang in his brain,
  And thrilled his spirit through.

Then in the flower-jeweled grass
  The strong man hid his face,
And One who stood from sight drew near
  And filled the green-roofed place
With that sweet spell repentance learns,
  And blessed him with its grace.

   .   .   .   .   .

That night the pirate's ship set forth,
  But never overtook
The prize they sought, for storms arose
  That the swift cruiser shook
Just like a thing with new-known fright
  That all her crew partook.

Some swore it was a wicked power,
  Their "evil day" at last,
For raving winds with blackest rains
  And blinding spray swept past,
Until they drove the rover's ship
  On shore, a wreck at last.

But there was one who murmured not,
  But, like the prisoned bird
Whose cage is broken, gladly wings
  His flight to where is heard
The notes of freedom; so his heart
  With gratitude was stirred.

   .   .   .   .   .

The days grew into weeks, and then
  One night there softly came
Near to a vine-wreathed cottage door
  A man of rugged frame,
But something in his earnest eye
  That might your wonder claim.

He halted, for a flock of birds
  Fed where a woman stood.
You would not say, "How beautiful!"
  But whisper, "Saintly good,"
For sorrow's sign was in her face—
  Perhaps of widowhood.

When all had fled and flown away,
  She turned with gentle sigh:
"Ah, where art thou, my fairest dove?
  The sad, long years go by,
And still I wait thy coming home
  To bless me ere I die."

A step—she turns and reads his face,
　Then takes his strong, rough hand.
No matter! 'tis her boy again;
　Her heart can understand;
And clear his eyes and smile as when
　He left his native land.

Oh, little doves on lonely isle,
　Ye did a wond'rous deed;
Ye saved his soul and cheered her heart
　That hungered with its need!
And more! ye blessed the wide, bright world,
　Where men and women read;

For, through all years of after life,
　He studied nature's page;
With brush and pen he wrought till men
　Loved him and named him sage.
Who hath such stores from nature won
　As the great artist, Audubon!

Nellie's Birthday Party.

My dear sister was promised a party on her approaching birthday, when she would be eight years old. Nellie had a particular friend whose name was Lina, and she also was to have a birthday festival, and as their anniversaries were but a few days apart, there was prospect of an unusual amount of joyousness within a short period.

These close companions were like and unlike each other. Both were fair and sweet-tempered. One night as we all came home from school together, our

NELLIE'S BIRTHDAY PARTY.

mother was at Lina's, and we waited while ma made ready to go home.

Lina asked, "Ma, what day is my birthday?"

The mother looked up in a surprised way and answered, "Dear child, I forgot—it has passed." Well, our surprise and Lina's disappointment were great.

The poor little girl cried bitterly, until ma said, "Never mind, Lina, you can have your party in with Nellie's, and it will be all the grander." Nellie, who was wiping her eyes in sympathy with Lina's grief, now brightened up and was perfectly willing. For fear that the other occasion might have the fate of a postponement, the time was counted and it was found that "day after to-morrow" was the happy day. As Lina was too timid and Nellie thought that "if a person was going to have anything they hadn't ought to have the trouble themselves, somebody else ought to do it for them," it was decided that upon me should fall the honor of issuing the invitations to those who attended our school, and on the way home visit the scattered families that were to be favored. Now, as my dear sister was very popular, and had once been unanimously elected, without a dissenting vote, and crowned Queen of May, it may be easily understood that I should have much walking to do, beside meeting the looks of slighted friends, for there had to be a limit. Perhaps this was one reason why Nellie declined being on the committee of invitations; but I am sure that the greater motive was her feeling that the honor and dignity of the occasion would be better sustained by her being entirely a recipient. Lina generously offered to stay home from school and help ma in the busy preparations, and also on the day itself. Dear, good little heart! In this she was unlike Nellie, who, with absorbing interest, watched all that was being done, in quiet admiration, while Lina's executive abilities and quickness of ideas seemed to brighten and accelerate as the day went on. When I returned at sundown, Lina took me to the pantry and cellar with whispers of pride. Then my share of labor began.

Ah, how many roses and other sweet flowers I gathered for bouquets, and how many yards of garlands, of arbor vitæs, feathery asparagus and long ferns, to decorate mantels, windows, and doorways! It took part of next morning too. "Very beautiful, my dear child," said father, taking a survey of it all just before he went down town to the office. "Very nice of you to do all in your power to honor your sister. Well, well, dear little Nellie, she's a good child! I'm very happy with you both. Good-by." It was warm weather, the fourth of August; so, early in the morning, to escape the heat, the guests began arriving, some bringing a little token, book-mark, ribbon, or tiny toy, but all were welcome alike, those who did and those who didn't.

Ma announced that it was Nellie's and Lina's party together. Nellie sat among the guests, but Lina was flitting here and there, waiting on the girls put away their things, then out in the dining-room, coming around corners with playthings,—everywhere was Lina. The warm and thirsty guests were waited upon with slight refreshments before beginning the pleasures of the day, and before long everything had found

its level. All the paraphernalia of doll house-keepi;
was brought out, and several sets of house-keepers ·
tablished upon the verandas and under trees. It w;
like a doll conference, so many had been brought alor.
I can't say how many bunches of grapes and cups '
sugar were used in making pies to be baked in Nellic
little stove, nor how many eggs were beaten to be ma
into uneatable cakes. Even the toy wash-tubs we
brought out and doll's clothes laundried to an astoi
ishing extent, but all were happy.

The next thing was a serenade from the boys, wh
had been gone somewhere a long time and now r
turned with a great flourish—hats decorated wit
rooster tail feathers, corn flowers and plumy grasses
pipes and piccolas whittled from willows, pumpkin
vine trumpets of all sizes and tones, and an indescrib
able instrument made of a split stick and green grass
A real drum had been brought from town, swords an
daggers hastily made from the lumber pile, beside
pop-guns, jew's-harps and harmonicas. What a nois
they made, and how they enjoyed themselves! Th
"martial band" having first charmed and then almost
distracted their hearers, and being requested to "g
off somewhere out of hearing," decided upon a change
and brief rest.

It was suggested that in harmony with playing
"keep house," some domestic animals were needed,
and one boy volunteered to be tied up under a tree or
all fours to represent a horse. This proved to be a
very restless, kicking animal. Another personated a

cow, not forgetting vicious shakes of the head and howling for an imaginary calf.

When the tying up became irksome, the horse broke his rope and ran away. Hammocks were swung under the trees, ball and kite playing and soap-bubble blowing followed.

What first occurred to mar the felicity of the scene was never fully understood. It was said ambiguously that "*some* had acted too smart." Presently there was a dignified redressing of dolls and other mysterious movements, and before those in the house knew what was going on, remarks of this kind were exchanged: "Yes, you'll never see my face again." " I don't want to see it or you either." " You think you're so fine!" "Yes, you've been cutting pa's pumpkin vines all to pieces and our willow trees, too, for your old trumpets and whistles." All this while the dinner was being prepared with great care and proper magnitude.

When ma came out to announce dinner, a scene of silence and desolation presented itself. Toys lay in disorder, and Nellie sat in silent dignity alone upon the spot where awhile ago had thronged and frolicked her guests. "Where are the children?" " Gone home."

The hired man was summoned and dispatched down the road to gather up and bring back the offended company. He found them, some resting by the way-side, others plodding wearily along in the hot sun. He succeeded in bringing them back, and they were led to where fresh water and towels abounded, and, thus refreshed, were marshaled into the dining-

room.   Here all feeling was soon dissipated, and when
dinner was over, the tables were cleared away, and
dancing began.   Before sundown the happy company
again started homeward, this time perfectly satisfied
with the pleasures of the day.

Would you like to know where all those little friends
are now?   One, I know, is a telegraph operator, another a well-known missionary.   One of them has a
great farm, where the mowing-machines cut a swath
a mile long before turning back.   Albert went to the
war, and laid down his life while leading his troops.
Eddie went with his father, who was appointed orni-
thologist to Maximilian in Mexico, and was drowned
in a bayou.   Many are scattered, I know not where.

But dear little Lina!   Sometimes, when coming
home from school, her face would turn pale, and the
tears run down her cheeks as she faltered on the way,
with pain.   Some called them "growing pains," and
said they would not last long.   We used to make a
chair with our hands and carry her along, resting now
and then.   By and by Lina could not go to school
any more, but sat at home in a reclining chair, patiently whiling away the time of taking medical treatment by doing such pretty work and studying, trying
to keep up with her class.   But the time came when
the pain would not let her think of anything else but
suffering.   Then her father traveled with her from one
place to another, spending hundreds of dollars, all in
vain.   Dear little Lina grew to look more like spirit
than human, so lovely were the long curls falling upon

her shoulders and bosom ; but those blue eyes were so large and sorrowful, one had the heartache to just look in them. One day the gentle spirit took its flight, and all was gone but the memory of Lina.

And Nellie? She grew to be a woman, and had a home and lovely children. She lived to labor in a holy temple, and gave back to the heavenly Father three lovely babes. She has followed them, and no doubt Nellie and Lina have met in that beautiful world where dwell the saints who kept the faith unto the end.

What a Little Girl Could Do.

FAR away in England a family was bowed in sorrow and want. The father had died, and there was a good-sized family to be provided for. The eldest children could get work away from home, just enough to provide for themselves. At home there were three more for the mother to toil for, the eldest only six. One day a little friend said to her: "Elizabeth, I have a place to work, but my time is nearly out, and I'm going home; but I think my mistress would take you if you would like to go." "Oh, thank you! I'll go with you now and find out about it." When they reached the house, the lady, in answer to the introduction and explanation, said, "You are so young and small, how could you wash my dishes?" "I would

stand upon a box." "You might break them while
putting them away." "No, ma'am, for I would be so
careful that it could not happen." "What would keep
you from being homesick?" "To know I was helping
mother." "Are you not afraid I might scold you?"
"Not if I do right, ma'am." The lady was so pleased
she called to see the mother, who, after many sorrow-

ful feelings, and
the kind assur-
ances of her vis-
itor, who was
well known, con-
sented to the
offer. Once a
week Elizabeth
saw her mother,
and at the end of
the year her kind
employer paid
her the full sal-
ary, and a boun-
tiful allowance

WHAT A LITTLE GIRL COULD DO.

of clothing and books, for Elizabeth had expressed
a wish to attend school. This she did for one year,
and helped her mother all her hours out of school-
time. "Now," said Elizabeth (eight years old),
"after one year in school, I ought to study alone."
So she worked for small wages all day, and spent
her evenings at home in study, instead of playing in the streets. So she continued for ten years,

At a proper age Elizabeth married a good man, and by the earnings she had saved, helped her mother as well as herself to come to Zion.   The once poor little girl now rides behind her own horses, and looks from her door upon more than one hundred acres of land, their valued and happy inheritance in Zion.

I cannot help thinking that the spirit shown by the little girl, and her course in life as she grew older, must have won the approval and blessing of our heavenly Father.   I think that holy angels must have looked with tender care upon the little Elizabeth, who started out in life at six years of age, and bore up her simple prayers to the holy throne.

What a Baby Did.

PERHAPS you are thinking: "Well, what *did* a baby do? and what could it do but be either pretty and cunning, or just as cross as can be? and what is there wonderful about either?"   If that's what you're guessing, you're mistaken; for this baby that I mean did a great deal of good, more than some grown folks ever did in their lives.   When anyone shakes their head and looks out of their eyes as you do now, I know you've given up guessing.   All right.   I'll tell you what the baby did, and it's true.

This baby's parents were obliged to go to town twice every week to supply certain rich families with

tnose nice things which grow chiefly in the country.
What good would it do for city people to try to
raise green peas, turnips, water-melons, and velvety
peaches? Are there not boys everywhere who can
flatten themselves so thin that they can get through all
kinds of fences? and how many hatfuls of green peas
would you think a small boy can eat, or how many
raw turnips? And what perilous risks have not boys
dared in the pursuit of water-melons? And with what
sure aim they can sling a rock at a peach! These are
a few reasons why the production of such good things
are left to the country people. I'm not saying that
boys are all of them bad; the best boys I ever knew
had a weakening of the soundest sense of honor on
several points, and they are these: Fondness for water-melons, going fishing, shooting, and looking too
earnestly upon an apple orchard.

The weakness was in not checking the desire immediately, for temptation grows fast while one hesitates.
These acts may be called small transgressions, and
are often passed over lightly, but when one has
planted and toiled to produce a thing, another who
has not done anything toward it has no right to expect a share, unless by honorable means.

I'm quite sure of one thing, and that is, all boys
have a high respect for country gardeners, for they
will follow such a wagon as long as there is anything
unsold in it.

Just let a farmer fasten a stick upright on his wagon,
stick a red apple on top, and the crowd will gather.

If he throws out a few now and then, don't the boys cheer him and coax their mothers to buy of him? Don't they declare for him that those are "dandy apples"?

Well, just such appreciative boys and girls were away down in that crowded, dusty, hot city, waiting every week all summer long for the market gardeners' wagons to bring them a little of the freshness of the country by way of one good thing or another; and so, why not go and earn something?

But there was the baby not old enough to take care of himself, and the little sisters at home not able to do it, and what a hard time a poor baby would have all day long in that noisy city. So a friend said: "Leave Benny with us; we will be pleased to have a baby in the house, and he can have a quiet, cool time till you come home." So it was settled, and Benny was brought to spend the day; he always brought something along with him for his friends. Sometimes it was a pound of sweet butter newly churned and tasting of the clover and the dew, sometimes a fine melon; well, every time it was something good and just what was needed for the day.

Now, you can see that as these folks had no garden, Benny was a benefactor as well as a visitor. His disposition was so quiet, amiable, and lovely, that the family said he was almost too good, for he never fretted or demanded attention. The soft little arm around one's neck, his pretty little way of smacking his lips for a kiss, and his patient waiting for his parents' return, all endeared him to the family.

Now, if Benny had been a fretful baby, all this pleasant state of affairs would have been impossible. So
when I say, "what a baby did," you see it was not
anyone else's goodness, but the sweetness of his own
nature.

The nice things that came fresh from the hill-side
farm would have been no object if the baby had been
disagreeable. So it was the baby that did it all, and
he shall always have the credit. This little incident
shows us that no one is too small to be good and be a
blessing to those around.

When summer and fall are gone, and the wagon
stops no more for Benny to be lifted out and carried
into the house, how still it will be, missing him! Ah!
that makes me think of something else that the baby
did. The family became so used to keeping quiet on
Benny's day with them, that the laughing, romping
children grew into the habit of entering slowly, as
though he might be in there asleep. "I feel as though
Benny is here when he isn't here." Then they would
unconsciously smile at thought of him, and say, "He's
a dear little fellow, ain't he?"

Now who can say that Benny did not wield an influence, and if a baby possesses that much, you had
best consider, "How much influence have I, and of
what kind is it?"

Buttermilk.

MANY boys would be willing to earn money if it could be done in a genteel way and in fine clothing. Such opportunities are rare, and especially in the outskirts of a city.

You know that such trades as lime and brick-making are carried on outside of town. It also happens that there also is where farms and pastures abound. Perhaps you are wondering what connection there can be between a brick-yard and a pasture, but it is a natural and convenient one, I can prove.

Generally, the great strong men who work at such trades are also rough in manners and speech, and have also tastes and requirements quite different from those who lead lives that do not tire and irritate the body and mind.

When hot weather came on in a certain brick-yard, there were some men who began to think that water was not just the thing to quench thirst. Certainly the water that flowed near them was not cool and was a little brackish to the taste, so pretty soon somebody said he wished he had some strong beer to drink. Before long others thought so too, and the next thing that happened was the men grumbled more at the hot weather, a few began to get excitable, and some became weak and sick. Things looked discouraging, especially when one after another gave up work, until a small force was left.

One warm forenoon, a timid, smiling boy came among them and inquired if anybody around liked buttermilk. He very soon found out that the majority of them did, and wanted to engage that cooling drink for every day.

Our bright boy began to wonder if the sixteen cows at home in the wide meadow could furnish as much buttermilk as forty men could drink, for it really appeared as though a churnful would not go very far, and then the family did not churn every day, either. Instead of being ridiculed, as he perhaps feared, he found himself taking orders for buttermilk at such a rate that he said he would have to find out if he could get enough to supply the demand.

"No more beer for me if I can get such buttermilk," cried one, and "That's what I say," echoed another.

When Dan reported to his mother, she solved the problem. " Buy up all the buttermilk of our neighbors and take the road cart to collect and deliver it with." Dan tried her advice, and if you think he made a financial failure, just watch him drive into the yard and see the men meet him with their tin pails and hear them smack their lips. I noticed at the end of the week that Dan handed his mother a buckskin pocket-book that looked almost ready to give up trying to keep clasped. Of course, dimes, nickels and quarters make a great display of size, and are not "worth their weight in gold," but Dan's income is satisfactory, I judge, and then there are no twinges of conscience, as there would be if he was selling intoxicating drinks to the hard-working men. And, see here, Dan is doing a temperance work among those men, although nothing is said of it. Good for Dan, say I, and I know you think so too.

Now you see the connection between the dry brickyard and the green pasture, don't you?

His Birthright.

THE Scotch are noted for frankness of speech and a stern integrity of character.

A little story was told to me not long since by one who of right is an earl's daughter. Her grandfather was, by a mistake, deprived of his rightful title and estate. He became so indignant that he removed some distance to a small property, and from that time ceased all communication with them. He had his three sons taught a useful trade, blacksmithing in its various branches, and advised them that, as partners with each other, their interests would be best maintained, and they would be able to make an honorable and independent living. To them he related the story of injustice.

After he had passed from life, and his sons each had a family, the eldest son was one day visited by a distant kinsman, one well known for his fearless spirit and high sense of honor. When they had conversed some time as friends long parted, they began to trace out their family lines.

Lord A. asked this Lindsay if he did not intend to try to recover his rights. The blacksmith replied that it would be an expensive undertaking and a long affair, as his cousins would contest it as long as possible; and that he did not at present wish to neglect his business, or harass his mind with it. Lord A. then asked, "Could you trust me to look over your papers?" "Yes," said Lindsay, "I can trust you," and he delivered to him all the documents. After four days Lord A. returned and offered his influence and efforts to assist him. Lindsay shook his head, meditatively. "Then," said Lord A., "will you take (naming a large sum). "No!" firmly replied his kinsman. "We Lindsays are able to *earn* our living without selling our birthright. Let them hold our lands and rest uneasily as thieves and rascals should; it *is* ours and they know it." "Yes," said Lord A., "and if I had the right that you have, I'd ride through the castle gate and demand the keys, and none would dare deny me."

Perhaps the very course that Lindsay took, proved a blessing to his family. If he had recovered his rights, it is not likely that his daughter would, in that position in life, have ever heard from the lips of a Mormon elder the tidings of the Gospel. As it is, she alone of all her family has gathered with the Latter-day Saints to the mountain land, where the Temples of God are reared, and by correspondence with her kindred has induced some of them also to inquire into our religion and express a determination to sometime visit this famed city and wonderful people.

Always, when I think of my dear and aged friend, I think of her as an earl's daughter.

If we only knew the truth, there are many of noble birth among us in the disguise of humble life, but our Father knows them and what they have left for His truth, and gives them peace and joy, holding in His keeping for them when they have finished their mission, titles and estates that none can take away.

What a noble spirit and worthy of emulation! Latter-day Saints should feel the same way when temptations arise, whether from enemies or friends.

We should never barter a principle or inherited right for gold. Some of our blessings are ours to enjoy, but not to dispose of. Children, remember the story of the noble Lindsay, who preferred to continue a life of labor rather than relinquish his birthright and inheritance.

The Doll in Norway.

CHILDREN who have dolls and toys in abundance, supplied them by loving and indulgent parents, have no idea how few pleasures of the kind are enjoyed by those of their own age in far-away lands, among the poor class, who never own a home, a horse or a cow. I have had good women tell me many domestic stories that made me feel sorrowful for the poor in their country, especially for the little children, for it seems only natural and right that their early years should be blessed with happy hours of innocent enjoyments free from care.

One sister told me how in her childhood she had to help all she could, and that an hour once a week was a holiday for her. Dolls were very scarce where she lived. She had heard of fine ones at the house where her mother worked two days in the week, and one of her associates had a very plain doll, but dearly appreciated. One day a kind woman gave my friend a doll with head carved out of wood and painted with strong-smelling paint, but that did not matter in the least, she was overjoyed. Christine made a little house out of a box for her doll to sit in before her, out in the yard, while she picked over wool or did other tedious work. The sight of Hilma dressed so finely made her feel as though she had company, and beguiled the long hours of weary labor. If Christine sometimes carried on a conversation with Hilma, no one ridiculed her, for she was an only child, and a lonely one too, because she seldom had a chance to associate with other children, except on Sundays, going and coming from church, or on some grand festival-day. Her mother, grandmother and aunt would often pause, listening to her chatter to her doll, and smile because she was happy. Very often poorer children would look through the fence with wistful eyes and then go slowly on.

One afternoon, about sundown, Christine was called to go on an errand. She promptly obeyed, looking back, smiling at Hilma as she passed out of the gate. Christine was kept waiting a while, and when she reached home the doll was not thought of immediately. But before bed-time Christine ran out to her neglected darling to find it gone. Pitiful cries and calls for assistance, long and repeated search, were all in vain. Christine sobbed herself to sleep, and many a sorrowful day of lonely toil passed in the little yard thereafter.

"But did you not get another doll?" I asked her. "No, we were too poor to spend money that way. I never had another doll in all my life, and I have no children to be excuse for me to buy one now." Christine finished her story so seriously that I could see well enough the great loss it had been to her.

Think of this, you little children who break toys and can get new ones in their places.

I know a little Norwegian girl who has not been long in Utah, and, so that her relatives at home might know how well she stood the journey, her auntie took her to have her photograph taken. Mary's aunt had given her a fine doll on the evening of her arrival, and the little one begged that she might have it in her arms, "For," said she, "they will see how rich you are, and how kind to me, when they see this beautiful doll in my arms." Mary's request was laughed at but granted, and she was more anxious to have justice done to the doll's features than her own; but the relatives saw a very happy face, too, for Mary's pride and joy could not be concealed.

To ride behind uncle's own horses; to see milk skimmed and butter made from uncle's own cows, and drink all the milk she wanted; to drive up the ewes and their pretty frolicking lambs into the pen at night; to feed the bewildering flock of chickens and pigeons of all sizes and kinds—all this seemed like immense wealth to little Mary. She could never do too much for her kind relatives who had brought her and her widowed mother to this wonderful country.

There are just as rich persons in Norway as in other countries; but I am telling you about the poorer ones, so that your own simple blessings may be better realized, for the poor in the Old World are almost certain to remain so all their lives, instead of rising to comfort and perhaps wealth, as the poor can do in our glorious America. A great man in England called America " God's gift to the poor." We should never forget this, but if there are those who do not know of the difference between this and other countries, and cannot go from home to see for themselves, just let them ask our foreign friends about it, and they will learn many valuable truths, and will then love more and more the country and their religion.

Another Party.

NOT many years ago I had my enjoyment watching a group of children playing "keep house." They made their play-house between the front door and four poplar trees on a pretty grass plot. There were Zina C. and her brother Allen, Zina M. and her brother Freddie and their little sister Ethel two years old.

Zina M.'s grandma had given them some nice cold tongue and ham, a teacup of flour and one of sugar. Zina C. contributed an egg, some milk and raisins and the use of her ma's cook-stove. The two Zinas brought out their dolls, tea-sets and furniture, besides borrowed rugs and curtains from their mothers, and the little play-house looked quite interesting, the cat and dog entering into the whole with as much zest as the others.

But the cooking! Zina C. was rolling out pie-crust in the tray of an old trunk, from which the paper kept coming off. The table was all set before the cooking was begun. Zina M. was mixing the cake in a rusty tin wash-basin, and Allen was vigorously beating the white of an egg and sugar for frosting. Isabel, the hired girl, was frequently asked if the oven was hot, and to please grease pie-plates and cake-tins for the baking. What a good time they were having!

Grandma M., Isabel, and somebody else were looking on through the window, and laughing at what they could see. Pretty soon the two Zinas saw it too. "Freddie's eating the raisins!" "Allen's licking the frosting off the spoon! I saw him. Oh, it's most all gone!" These ungentlemanly assistants (three and six years old) were dismissed from the service and told to "sit down and behave till dinner-time."

Well, when these peculiar pies and cakes were done,

Isabel and the grandmas were laughing till their sides ached, and wondered if the children could eat them, when a loud scream drew their attention to the play-house again. The dog and cat were helping themselves to the meat and butter. Just outside the trees, quietly resting his arms on the fence and enjoying the scene, stood a benevolent-looking gentleman, his face all smiles. "Isn't that the Bishop?" whispered Isabel. The impatient dog and cat were properly slapped and scolded and dinner proceeded. Little Ethel drank all the milk at once, Freddie grabbed the raisin cake before it was sliced, the two Zinas reached to recover it, and in doing so Allen's chair was tipped over backward till his struggle upset the table. Just then I saw the smiling old gentleman hurrying down the sidewalk laughing to himself as though something delightful had happened and wiping his eyes as if for very joy.

Singing in the Orphan Asylum.

FEW children in Utah have ever heard of an orphan asylum, and it is likely to be a long while before they will see one here, because in our domestic system there are always relatives to take care of those who lose one or both parents. It is, in one sense, a melancholy sight to see a large building, and know that it is an institution of that kind; it is sad to go through its rooms, and know that all those bright, youthful

beings, formed to love and to be loved, are passing
days and months in a life that lacks its most needful
blessing, family ties. A sense of loneliness, restraint,
and longing seems to pervade the whole. They may
outgrow the heart-hunger, and go on without it, but
that life lacks its best part after all.

Again it is a great blessing that the homeless can
be gathered in where shelter, warmth, food, clothing,
instruction, and guardianship are all provided. All
honor and blessing to those noble and gentle spirits
that take a mission upon themselves to care for the
helpless. There must be a great deal of love and patience in their hearts.

When I was a little girl, my mother took me with
her to visit the Protestant Orphan Asylum in San
Francisco. She was one of the founders and direct-
ors. The sixty orphans were seated as in school, and
a program entertainment was given to show what they
had been learning. Articles made by both sexes were
shown. I remember above all others there a girl who
sat in a large chair, in which, it was said, she passed
day and night. Some dreadful affliction had made
her a cripple, and her hair was all gone, so that she
wore a soft silk cap over the bandages on her suffering
head, and she could not use her hands; but they said
she was so good and patient they all loved her, and
tried to cheer her sad life. While we were there, they
sang a song about a poor mother alone in the dark
with her dying son, while across the street was a
mansion brilliantly lighted, where dancing and feast-

ing went on. It was called "The Watcher." O
children, think of it! I have known of a case where
the only light in the sick room, was from the fire-place.
This seemed hard enougl.. I often went to the asylum, but those visits were all sad recollections. One
dear little boy was told that an uncle was coming to
take him to his grandparents. He was so sweetly
hopeful about it, and the others all thought him so
fortunate; but the ship encountered a storm, and the
good uncle was drowned. When the news of this
second calamity came, no one was willing at first to
bear the sad tidings to the dear boy. After some
months a reliable friend was found who could take
him to his own relatives, and that friend was a good
old sea captain, going home. Not a woman was on
board the ship, but a letter from the "old folks"
proved that he reached there all right. Strange to
say, no one ever claimed any of the rest, for whole
families had been destroyed by the cholera, with the
exception of these few children. It must be very sad
for any person to feel that he stands alone upon the
earth, the last of his family.

Deaf and Dumb.

THE child who is possessed of the five senses, seeing, hearing, tasting, smelling, and speech, and has a
well-formed body, is greatly blessed, though lowly and

11

poor, whether he knows it or not. To be a cripple i
an affliction; to inherit a sickly body is a serious bar
rier to enjoyment. Then how thankful children shoul
be who have sound bodies and all their faculties! Im
agine a watch or a sewing-machine with one or mor
parts missing! There are so few cases among the
Latter-day Saints of physical or mental deficiency that
our children cannot realize how it is out in the world.
If we placed a proper value upon these gifts of God,
we would never use them unwisely.

We would not lend our eyes to gaze upon forbidden
pleasures (gambling, horse-racing, evil company) or
books, such as by false teaching or fascinating stories
lead the mind astray; our ears to listen to calumnies,
profanity, or impure conversation; our tongues to
speak falsely, or taste intoxicating drinks, or tobacco,
or in saying anything we should be ashamed of.

In resisting these temptations lies the chief trial of
life. "What!" asks one, "do the chief evils of life
come through the use of eyes, ears, and tongue? I
thought it was what we did." Yes, but your eyes,
ears, and tongue lead you into the acts. The souls of
the blind are unsullied by sights of sin. The hearts of
the deaf have never ached in response to angry tones.
The tongues of the dumb have never uttered pro-
ianity.

When I have heard and seen children quarreling, with
discordant voices, and darting angry looks as chal-
lenges or resentment, I have wished that I might take
them to an institution where the deaf, dumb, and blind

eside. I think their hearts would be touched with
pity and sorrow.

Look upon the eyes that have never seen one of the
millions of beautiful things in this world, the ears
that have never heard music or a loving voice—
that exist in eternal blank. Think of the tongues like
frozen brooks, fettered prisoners that cannot utter one
sound, though in peril or the pains of death. Try to
realize such a life as this would be, or all of these
combined, and then ask yourself if God has slighted
you.

But the fortunate possessor of all these gifts must
not be too sure that they are his, or his to keep ; they
are not; God has lent them to us, and requires us to
make a wise use of them.

Some have kept these blessings all their lives, but I
have known of instances to the contrary. In two
cases, where falsehood and abuse had been exercised,
the parties were for several days before death unable
to speak. Tears and anguish of the countenance told
plainly of the soul's punishment, but the words of repentance could not then be spoken ; it was too late!
There have been many instances of God's visitation
and judgment. O children of the Latter-day Saints,
you have been taught of the watch that is over you by
day and by night! Shun such dangers, and live in
such a manner that you may feel a right to claim the
blessing and protection of the heavenly Parent.

Dumb Creatures.

WHEN the all-wise God created animals, and som
of them for the use of man, it is not to be believe
that he intended creatures of the highest degree o
intelligence to be cruel to those so much inferio
in understanding and so helpless. When men figh
it is considered cowardice for one to strike anothe
when he is down. (Gentlemen never fight, they rea
son the matter to an understanding and settlement
But man will strike poor dumb animals, who are al
the time down in helplessness. A gentleman neve
does this wrong to his honor, for he knows there ar
other ways of doing. Man would soon weary of th
many heavy burdens, or sink under them, if he and no
the horse had to bear them. There would be fe
journeys made, and where would be the delightfu
rides and sleighing were there no horses? In som
countries men transport great loads of freight upo
their backs, and how strange it looks to us, even i
pictures.

Cows are generally timid creatures, and, in a certai
way, the best of animals. How many good things t
eat would be lacking if we had no milk! Nothing i
the vegetable kingdom would answer the purpos
The cow, then, should at all times be regarded as ou
benefactress as much as man is hers, and should re
ceive our kindest treatment. What would the chil
dren do without bread and milk? How some folk

would miss ice-cream in the summer-time! And then such frolics as the children have in the country with bossy's calf.

But aside from our own ideas and pleasure on the subject, we have a Master who is the friend of all dumb creatures, and some day we and they will meet Him and have to listen to what will be said.

In the Bible it is written: "And at His coming all flesh shall speak, and the trees shall clap their leaves for joy." All flesh includes animals, birds, and every other living thing. How will some persons feel in the day of judgment when the dumb creatures they have beaten or half starved rise up before them and bear witness against them? The Creator is just, he will hear the helpless, and he will not say, "Your cause is just, but I can do nothing for you;" no, those cruel hearts will have to meet their reward.

It seems to me that a person who will take two peaceable dogs and worry them into a cruel fight, is not even of so good a spirit as the dogs themselves. It is strange that human intelligence can stoop to such a level, no, beneath the level of the brute creation.

Cruelty to animals is receiving a large share of attention in some cities, and laws to protect these dumb creatures and punish their cruel masters, have been enacted. There is an association which publishes a good paper called *Our Dumb Animals*, and it is a good one for everyone, old and young, to read. Many thousands of children are joining it by letter. Its object is to teach kindness, and thus the law become natural and universal. Many beautiful stories are related, and they desire to learn all they can of such in the experience of their new members.

In a certain kingdom, Norway, I am told that if a man beats his horse cruelly, or overloads it, or drives it too fast, he is brought before the proper officers of the law and fined. If the offense is repeated, he is fined and imprisoned, and on the third offense these penalties are again imposed and the animal taken from him. But in that country it is seldom that cruelty is exercised, for it is hard for the poor to earn a living, and a horse or a cow is regarded as riches, and these creatures are generally treated with all the kindness they need. Sheep are also very kindly treated, for the nice long wool will some day be transferred from its own place into the family's use.

I have even seen a bed-spread made from cow's hair, and it was a handsome one, too. I knew a young girl who told me: "In my country I was poor and could not afford to keep a pet hen, even, times were so hard. Now I keep sixty. I am rich." This girl made a good use of her income, and in two years' profits of her industry, emigrated a lone relative, who now unites with her in the same business. These good women saw much among us Americans that looked to them like waste. A friend once remarked: "These foreigners use what we would waste, and sell what we would use, and that is why they prosper where we do not get ahead." I once saw a Swede currying his horse and observed that he carefully saved

the hair in a box. As a dear friend of mine says,
"I haven't got a particle of inquisitiveness, but my
'want to know' is very large," so I asked him why
he did that. He told me that he was going to add a
room to his house before long, and would use this in,
the plaster instead of throwing it away and buying
more. Then he patted his horse and praised its shining coat and ended by thanking Blackbird for the con-
tribution.

Robbing Bird'snests.

IT is quite common in the spring of the year for
boys to go out on expeditions for young birds. The
brown larks that make their nests low in the grass, and
the magpies that build theirs in clumps of scrub oak,
are the commonest victims. Many of you have never
seen a magpie's nest, so you will be surprised to learn
that it is very large, sometimes three feet across, and
has enough wood in it to make a bonfire. These
nests look quite coarse and uncomfortable, but who-
ever heard the birds complain? It may seem a beautiful idea to have a young bird to raise, but there is
more sorrow than beauty in it. I have seen so many
of these poor things brought away from their parents
that it seemed likely to clean out the tribe; but the
saddest feature is the cruelty practised by slitting their
tongues to enable them to talk. As I have known

many birds to die from this mutilation (not being able
to talk), I have often wished that it could be prevented.
There was one case near by where the poor parent-
bird hovered outside, pitifully answering the plaintive
cries of her wounded and prisoned young one, which
was worried by a pet dog, watched by a hungry cat,
and sadly neglected by its captors, until death released
it.

At another time I was walking, on a hot, dusty day,
in Salt Lake City, when, coming to a second-hand
store, I saw, in a small cage, a poor magpie panting
with the heat and hopping to and fro, vainly seeking
to make its escape.

If I had had money with me, I would have bought
it away and loosed it among the wild trees.   Poor bird!
The sight made me sad at heart.   I would not have
that bird's suffering to answer for, for any price.

MOURNING DOVES.

When I was quite young, I heard a good neighbor
chiding his boys for robbing nests.   Said he: "My
brother and I robbed a mourning dove's nest of her
two young ones.   She followed us home, but we did
not mind her sad cries.   By and by we began to wish
she would stop, and one of us tried to frighten her away,
but she would come back.   We were so tired with our
ramble that our mother let us go to bed very early, and
as we fell asleep we heard her mournful voice.   Next
morning it was the first sound we heard, and all day it
continued.   We stuck to the birds, but by night began

to feel badly, still would not give them up. In the morning there it was again, and we could stand it no longer. We said we would take them back to her nest, but when we uncovered them they were dead. Oh, how sad and frightened we were! My brother thought that if we put them where the mother could see them she would understand and go away, so we laid them on the roof of the porch and came away. She had been watching us and settled beside them, continuing her sad notes. This seemed worse than ever, so we climbed up again and carried them away to some tall grass, hoping she would follow and stay there ; but no, that mother-bird flew back and forth, cooing her broken-hearted story of accusation until she died.

"We never robbed another bird's nest, and I never hear a mourning dove now, that I do not feel sorry for that deed." Mr. Garner wiped his eyes as he concluded, and you may be sure we all felt pretty solemn.

THE ROBIN AND THE CARPET RAG.

I will tell you something not so sad. Do you think birds understand anything we say ? "Well," you answer, "some birds, tame ones, may, if they've been taught." That is true; but a lady once told me something so curious that I could not say anything against it and yet—it was very strange.

She had been sewing carpet-rags out on her porch, and it was about the time of spring for birds, especially robins, to be building their nests. As she sat all alone at her quiet work, she noticed the lively movements of a robin which seemed to be also watching her.

This interested the lady, and she kept very still, as she continued her sewing. By and by the bird came near enough to seize a long soft rag that had fallen just over the edge of the porch. Mrs. Robin tugged very hard, pulling it along backwards for some distance, when she stopped for a rest, still eyeing the lady.

"Oh, you little thief!" said she softly, "stealing my carpet rags." The bird looked at her, then at the rag, and to her surprise flew a little distance away and sat for a while on the fence as though not knowing what to do.

The lady said she began to feel as though the bird had understood her, and said she: "There that bird sat and sat and I watched her, and she watched me till at last I felt so mean I was ashamed of myself, although I only said it in fun; but at last I spoke, " Come and get it, you pretty bird; you can have all the carpet-rags you want. And what do you think? As true as I live, that robin flew back and got that carpet-rag and came for some more I threw over while she was gone, and I tell you I felt relieved." Now, whether the bird understood words or not, this circumstance really occurred.

At our home in the country we watch the birds with great interest, although there are not so many or such pretty ones as in California, my early home.

When we see large flocks of blackbirds flying low,

we look for high winds. Sometimes they seem to hold "conference" in a large locust tree near by, and then we have some fine choir exercises between the remarks of the leaders. I am sorry to have to state that these meetings are sometimes broken up by a mob-like attack of boys with guns.

We have the mischievous little English sparrows, the little brown snow-birds, and, oh! when the first flock of bluebirds comes in the spring, how glad we are, and throw out wheat in the front yard! It is a lovely sight to see one's snow-covered yard adorned with a flock of lovely bluebirds with top-knots.

We have read that they are very fond of the berries of the Virginia creeper, and as we have a fine one, that was a slip taken from the beautiful vine at the Wells House, on the corner opposite the Deseret News Office, we have expectations of annual visits from this regiment in blue uniform.

We value our vine very highly, first, because of where it came from, second, on account of its own beauty, and third, on account of the bluebirds.

Is it not a vine of more than ordinary interest?

The next birds we welcome are the robins; they are regarded as a sure sign of spring, but they will insist on moving so close to the cherry trees. But, after all, perhaps the Lord intended cherries for birds as well as for persons, and we must not be selfish.

Then there are the larks. I know a boy who wants to spend a day in the country just to hear the larks sing, and I don't wonder.

Very soon there is a rush of others, all building in
the orchard and lucerne fields. If you want a treat,
slip down into a field where larks, blackbirds and bob-
olinks have colonized for the summer. Just lie down
with the tall blades and green plumes of wheat, rye or
barley around you, and listen for an hour or two. If
new happiness does not slip into your soul, then I
think the gates of it must be fastened, the lock rusted
and the key lost.

If you live in a city where such a delight as this
cannot be had, tame birds are better than none; but I
would rather walk down the green aisles of a corn-
field whose blades are like swords, whose tassels are
like silk floss, and whose very rustle betokens the industrious, bustling farmer, hurrying up his crop for
the mill. Perhaps when you get down to the farther
end, a whole army of sunflowers with their splendid
golden heads will surprise you, and some common
weeds may be all interlaced with the dodder, as
though a skein of yellow silk thread had got tangled
in them. But if you must live in the city, which of
those birds that live in cages do you like best? I have
had parrots, cockatoos and canaries, but my favorites
were the humming-birds, and I will tell you about
them. One day while walking in the orchard, I observed a large knot on a branch. As I gazed, a humming-bird flew out, and, stepping up, I found a nest
not near so large as half a common egg, and in it were
two eggs like peas. What a wonderful sight for me!
and a good long look I enjoyed every day.

One morning when I went there I saw two black, ugly things, and exclaimed: "Oh, those horrible bugs have eaten those pretty eggs!" and was just going to send them whirling, when they opened their mouths, and I saw that they were young birds, but such ugly things. I watched them daily, and they grew very fast, their bodies soon catching up in proportion to their mouths, and in due time the pretty feathers appeared. Then I took a hoop-skirt, covered it with mosquito bar netting, gathered together at the top and underneath, and, hanging it in a deep window, had a large and pretty cage. I cut off the apricot branch and fastened it like a perch inside, then with fresh bunches of sweet flowers in the swinging vase, it was a pretty home. I wondered if the old birds would have me for a landlady, and left the front open. It was not long before they flew to their young ones, and then the opening was fastened. I afterward hung a division inside, and other humming-birds also came in. In a short time all were so tame that they would perch on one hand and eat from a spoon held in the other, and when they were done eating the dissolved sugar or honey, they would wipe their long bills on my hand. They also beame very affectionate, and when a hand was thrust inside, they would fly to it, and, perching, rub their heads against it just as a kitten does. Visitors were often surprised at these lovely pets and their humming. One was a voracious and noisy fellow, and I let him go, for his incessant darting and loud humming sometimes made our heads ache.

Once after a thunder-storm I found some dead humming-birds and happened to throw them near an ant-
hill. A few days later I discovered them entirely
stripped of feathers and skin. Once when I was holding a live one by the feet and its wings were extended,
its feathers seemed to stand out, and I could see almost through the body, which appeared like a bubble,
so I thought they have hardly any flesh upon them.
Well, the ants had left the skeletons entire, from bill-
tips to claw-tips, and they were the tiniest and prettiest anatomies that could be imagined. I kept them a
long time as curiosities, in a pretty, saucer-shaped
shell.

California has one hundred varieties of these tiny
birds. I have seen them perched upon clothes-lines,
and so tame that the gardener could strike the line
with his hoe handle, when they would drop, stunned
by the shock. They are also very wise and wary.
One cold morning I found one that was like dead. I
held it by the tip of its bill, pitying the limp little creature, then laid it in my hand, admiring the pretty feathers, when, away it flies! "Oh, the little deceiver!"
cried my sister. But perhaps it just then, in the
warmth of my hands, recovered consciousness.

On cool mornings I often wore a soft woolen scarf
around my shoulders, crossed in front and tied behind, especially in my early rambles before breakfast.
More than once I found, after a rain, chilled humming-
birds unable to fly. It was easy to catch these, for
they were just newly fledged, and I would place them

inside my warm scarf. Before long they would begin
to flutter; then when I reached home it was easy to
add them to my collection. I fear that many of those
fairy-like creatures die annually if a cool wave occurs
before they are grown.

A PARROT.

Now let me tell you of a parrot I once knew. He
was owned by the mayor of San Francisco, who lived
so near to the ships in the harbor at one time that
the sailors could be seen on the ships, and their rough
language heard by Polly, who seemed to be always
listening to everything, and to have no objection to
repeating it. I found this out by following the housekeeper into the kitchen, when I was at the house with
my mother. Polly had become so boisterous that his
society was not considered suitable for the parlor.
They called Polly "him" and "her" also. Polly
often annoyed the cook by moving the spice-boxes
and other small articles he was using, if he turned his
back, blowing out the wax candles in the dining-
room with his wings, disarranging the newly-set table,
etc. Polly would call back the master's hound from
following him, or cry, "Stop thief!" after any gentleman passing. When Polly at last caught a gentleman's gold-bowed spectacles from beside his book
while he was opening their case to put them away,
and then dropped them from the balcony into the harbor, patience was exhausted, and Polly banished from
the luxurious home. After this I never saw Polly
again.

WHEN about eight years old, I had, on my way to school, to pass three things that I dreaded. One was a lone pelican that would follow me for a portion of my school lunch. I judge that it could easily have swallowed it all and wished for more.

The next was a lame old white horse that would walk when I walked and run when I ran. He was a constant alarm to me, although he might once have been a pet and his intentions may have been friendly. Perhaps some little girl just my size may have been good to him and he remembered it; but I didn't know. Further along lived a gentleman who had as pets four monkeys, and they used to climb the poles to which they were chained and then jump down and make disagreeable faces and noises, beside throwing anything they could get hold of at passers. I have never liked monkeys since.

Cats and Kittens Crossing a Swamp.

IN some parts of California, Indian labor used to be employed, and generally they made their wickings at a short distance from their employers' house, as they were pretty sure to be kept for several months if well behaved. These wickings were made of clean new rushes, and when leaving the farm they always burned them down, leaving no rubbish to mark where they

THE CAT THAT TRAVELED FROM THE STATES TO UTAH.

had been. Not all tenants are as thoughtful and neat as this. These Indian families were fond of dogs and cats. At our Indian quarters there was one cat that used to come every morning, cross a little swamp, crossing over one the rail fence that reached from one side to the other, for her breakfast. Instead of staying around and wearing out her welcome by getting into mischief, she always went home at a quick gait after her meal of milk and table scraps.

One very delightful morning when the birds had wakened me just at daylight, I remembered about and started out for some certain strawberries hidden away in a little dimple of a spot down a gentle slope, for I thought they would be ready by this time. While picking my way through the shortest of the grass, I heard piteous little mews and other cries, and looking around, to my surprise I saw the poor old cat in the grass, and in the trail she had made, one, two kittens struggling along in desperate dislike of the dew, which had made them look so miserable, while farther back, on the top rail of the fence, staggered, clung and mewed two more frightened kittens, who only knew that they were following their mother. She was already weary of running to and fro, coaxing her timid little ones along on their first journey; so I thought it only humane for the stronger to help the weaker, and, accordingly, went to meet those on the fence. But my "kitty, kitty" being in English was not understood by these Indian kittens, and they stopped, with elevated backs, enlarged tails, defiant spittings and backings, refusing my help. However, I kept on and captured them all, while the mother amply expressed her gratitude in ways plain enough to me. By the time she and the other two were in my apron, the berries were forgotten and the main idea was a box with bed and food.

They understood that well enough, and spent the day contentedly, but at night the mother took them all back to camp. You see she did not intend to forsake old friends for the new, unlike many persons whom prosperity blinds to their comrades in adversity. With next morning's light, I was out to see if the exploit was to be repeated, when, sure enough! there she came, her little ones following this time with more confidence. They continued their visits as long as they desired. I thought that poor mother showed the same maternal solicitude and provident care as the human mother in poverty does, when obliged to go forth and seek food for her little ones. When the camp broke up to leave in the fall, I saw among their effects the good old cat with her four kittens cozily perched among the luggage on the back of a pony which an Indian woman was leading. As the mother had traveled that way before, I suppose she had instructed her family that there was nothing to fear.

THE CAT THAT TRAVELED FROM THE STATES.

What would you think to see a cat that had traveled all the way from Illinois to Utah, in a wagon ? I suppose you have never asked the question, " Who introduced the first cats into Utah?" for of course you know they were not here always, like the coyote and the crows. I do not remember the name of the persons who did this kind service, but I can tell you the true story as it was told to me.

When a certain family left Illinois, a little girl hugged her pet in her arms, keeping it covered from sight until a long way from home. It was believed by her parents that kitty would get lost after a while and so trouble them no more, but she seemed to know that the safest place was with her little mistress, and never strayed from camp, but always climbed into the wagon before starting-time, and was soon purring herself to sleep. When the family reached Salt Lake City (then a wilderness), kitty was much older, and one day presented the camp with four fine specimens of her tribe. These were much admired, and, when old enough, were anxiously sought for in good homes. This renowned cat, the fondled pet and respected ancestress of Utah cats, met her untimely death by the bite of a snake.

About three years later a family who owned one of her descendants, moved to California, and a short time after presented my sister and I each with a handsome black and white kitten and an account of their interesting grandparent, the pioneer cat of Utah. We were very proud of these handsome pets, for they attracted much attention from their elegant appearance and gentleness.

Snip and Tom grew to the dignity of about twelve pounds each, and lived to be a little less than eighteen years of age.

Dick.

I KNOW that some children like dogs, so I will tell them about a fine one I once knew. He was very large, being of both New Foundland and St. Bernard breeds.

DICK.

There were no children in the family when Dick was brought home, and his master and mistress took pains to teach him many things. When supper was nearly ready, Mrs. Fair would say, "Dick, go find your master and bring him home." Off he would go at full speed and in due time return with Mr. Fair. It

seems that Dick would find his master, gently bark to
attract his attention, then take hold of his coat cuff,
which was understood by his master. Sometimes
when Mr. Fair would start to go up town, Mrs. Fair
would say, " Don't let your master go, Dick," and
the dog would keep close watch of every movement,
and when Mr. Fair would raise his hand to the hat-
rack, Dick would spring and pull it down. After
amusing themselves this way awhile, at a signal that
fun was over, Dick would relinquish his duties as guard.
What I most admired about Dick was his tending
baby.   There was a little child in one part of the house
and Dick helped it learn to walk.   Leo would catch
hold of the thick black curls and hold on, while Dick
would walk carefully along, watching the baby.   If
Leo began to stagger, Dick would carefully settle
down to the floor and let the baby fall on his shaggy
side.   Dick would rock the cradle while Leo slept,
and bark joyfully when he woke.   Many a gentle
romp they had together.   Leo soon learned to throw
a ball, which Dick would chase after and bring back.

By and by Mrs. Fair moved to another house,
and she thought Dick missed his little friend Leo.
He used to watch some little girls at play with their
dolls, and would get so interested and bark so loudly
that his mistress said she would make a large doll for
Dick and see what he would do; so she .dressed up
a chair cushion with a hood and an apron, and no one
could help laughing to see Dick's delight.   He would
play it was asleep, cover it over and watch it, then

pick it up and rush around making such a barking
and racket, for he was very large and heavy. When
Dick was tired of playing with his doll, he would lay
it in a certain little closet and turn the button of the
door with his nose. If, just for fun, anyone went to
the little door, Dick would growl as much as to say,
" That's mine, let it alone."

One day his mistress said to me, "I'm going to set
Dick to mind the steak; now you notice him." So
she called him and told him that she was going out of
the room, and if the meat began to smoke, to call her;
then she put it in the hot frying-pan and went out.
Dick sat in front of the stove and fixed his gaze upon
the meat, now and then practicing a few sniffs. Presently he snuffed more earnestly, gave a few low growls,
and as the odors and steam increased, he grew excited
and barked loudly. As his mistress purposely delayed
coming in, he ran out to her, caught her dress, and
began pulling her toward the stove. When Mrs. Fair
attended to the meat, Dick expressed his satisfaction
by a few barks and some jumps that made the dishes
rattle. She gave him his portion outside the door, and
told him he might go up town, which he presently did.
After a while Dick learned to sit on the driver's seat
and hold the lines in his mouth, or take a basket with
written order to the meat market and baker's. Dick
never loitered, but did his errands promptly, and never
touched the food he bought. Dick at last left Utah
with his master and traveled considerably among the
mines and miners, who all made friends with him.

The Pathetic Story of Madame Catalini.

To begin with, my friend, I am descended from an ancient family, and my ancestors, if numbered, would prove numerous enough to astonish you.

While still quite young, I was the favorite of the family in whose mansion my mother resided, and well remember the soft-cushioned chairs and sofas on which I frisked or reposed as inclination prompted, and the fringes, cords, and tassels with which I used to play. There were also work-baskets and boxes, containing every kind of device that would entertain a kitten of lively nature, pet dogs, and singing-birds; but my most pleasant playmates were the little master and mistress, who carried me in their arms, shared delicate morsels of food with me, and often rocked me to sleep. Thus my childhood was passed in-doors, with an occasional romp at butterflies (who looked as though they would taste delicious), with fluttering leaves, or a peek-a-boo game among the vines with my little human friends.

As I grew older, I had many admirers, but knew nothing of the sorrows of life. The first unpleasant surprise to my feelings was the way in which some of our visitors were treated, on the occasion of a serenade to myself. A singular-looking article, called a boot-jack, was hurled by a servant at Signor Tomcoto, a vocalist of great note in our neighborhood. The pro-

fessor luckily escaped injury, but the fine troupe of
singers was completely broken up, at least for that
occasion.

Several years passed after this event, during which
I learned many serious and important things, for I
gained quite an understanding of the human family,
on whose bounty we depended, and whose very expression of face and tone of voice mean so much to us.
I learned how they can pet us one week and go off on
a pleasure trip the next, leaving us shut up inside a
tight house, with no water to drink, and nothing to
eat but mice; and, oh, how lonesome a house can be
to a cat when the family are gone, and not even the
canary or parrot left for company!

I have known them to cruelly treat or even kill our
little ones, but we must not even scratch back.

I have heard them speak in a heartless tone of " fur
trimmings made from pussy's coat," but hardly understood what was meant; also something about violin
and guitar strings being made from some part of our
physical structure.

I once cautiously examined a guitar while my mistress was absent from the room, but I did not see anything about it that I could recognize, and when I
softly drew my paw across the strings, they made a
startling sound, and one snapped. When my young
master re-entered the room, he said, "This catgut
string is broken; let's have another." Now although
I do not understand exactly what he meant, I often
wonder how the change takes place between a cat and

a guitar string; it is one of the mysteries to me. Another thing. Why is the natural melody of a cat's own voice at night-time more objectionable than the sounds produced in an unnatural manner from an instrument that is, in some way, part wood and part cat, and to the sounds of which happy-hearted persons will listen with delight, or dance the hours away, keeping up such a disturbance that no cat can sleep long.

There goes a boy who always throws a stone at a cat, no matter how quiet she is. There is an old woman who would say "Scat!" in church if she dared, and there is a little girl in whose care I could trust my own kittens, and be happy. I will tell you something about her, and it is as true as anything ever was. One day, for some reason that I could not understand, her good mother reproved, and, oh! slapped her. My little mistress went and sat down in a corner, and was crying softly to herself, when my son Thomas gently approached her. After a moment he slipped into her lap, slid one paw and then another around her neck, and snuggled his head up close to her cheek. Little mistress felt the caress, and, knowing it was sympathy, clasped him in her arms, exclaiming, "O Tommy, you're the only friend I have in this world!" Then she rose up and walked away with him in her arms, and the next time I saw her the trouble was all over.

We animals have to be on our guard, and learn to study faces, for there are many kinds of persons.

I have heard my little master read of a cat who made her master rich, and he became Lord Mayor of

London-town. His name was Whittington, and he had her portrait painted, sitting on the arm of his chair. I have also heard of men who made books, and had cats for their favorite pets; but strangest of all, in a country named Egypt, they even worshiped them! However, ancient history is not my theme; the present time will suffice.

Why is it that ladies will patronize the killing of birds to get plumage for their hats, but blame us cats for killing common birds to feed our crying little ones? Young ladies ought to be more refined in sentiment than cats ought, and great strong men who could work ought to be above killing little birds by the thousand, I think; but then what amount of moralizing ever accomplished a reform when the wrong-doer was the strongest party? I feel that I must resign myself to my lot with all the patience I have, continuing thankful for my good home; but, oh, that I could speak to girls and boys, and ask them to be merciful to the helpless creatures that are willing to be useful when possible, and ready always to romp and play for their diversion!

At this point Madame Catalini seemed quite weary. It was a hot day in July, and everyone felt the effect. Madame Catalini arose and walked toward the kitchen stove, under which she stretched her languid frame, and resigned herself to repose. "Well," said cook kindly, "ain't it strange how a cat can sleep in a place like that this hot day? Now *I* would rather have gone into the cellar. Let her alone; she'll make the mice fly after that nap!"

How the Horse Was Persuaded.

NOT many days ago a gentleman told me a story which I think is so good I will tell it to you, and I hope that any of you who have the care of a horse will follow the example given. Said he: I was crossing a sandy ridge when I observed ahead of me a load of hay which the horses were vainly endeavoring to move. A man stood on one side with a stout stick beating one of the animals, but stopped just before I reached them. I asked, "Friends, what is the matter?" "We've been pounding this horse for not pulling, and we're going to take him out of the harness and pound him more." "See here, my friends, don't do that; let me advise you my way, and then if he won't pull, I'll take your load to the next town myself." The man looked surprised and asked, "What would you do?" "Give him a feed of oats, and after he has eaten them curry and brush him, then harness him to the load and start off as though nothing had happened." The man considered a moment as though he hated to do it, but finally answered, "Very well, I'll do it just to satisfy you, but I'm doubtful." We talked while the horse was eating, then we curried and brushed him, talked kindly in the meanwhile, then hitched onto the load again. The driver mounted, merely said, "Get up," in an ordinary tone, when, to his surprise (we helping on the hind wheels at the time

for a starter), the horses started off all right. "I'll
try your plan every time after this," said he. "If you
do, he'll be grateful for your kindness and do all he

KINDNESS ALWAYS WINS.

can for you in return." So they went along each with
a better opinion of the other, and *one* with the sense of
having avoided a great wrong and performing a good
part instead.

A JOKING HORSE.

Did anyone ever before hear of such a thing as a
joking horse? I never did until about four years
ago. I was enjoying the favor of what is, in my
neighborhood, called "a chance ride," that is, a ride
in your neighbor's and not your own conveyance.
The good brother placed me in the care of his two boys
for a ride from town home, and I can truly say that
it was a most enjoyable one, for I learned how manly
small boys may become through a life of industry and
business. These country boys had a great deal of
character and independence of spirit, that are truly
admirable and are very entertaining. Many a good
thing have I heard from these boys, who get up at
three o'clock in the morning to take their produce to
town; so, on this particular occasion, I listened to the
boys' narrations, and at last one of them remarked:
"These are both good horses, but they ain't nothing
like old Billy; he was the jokingest horse anybody
ever saw." This interested me, so I inquired what
kind of jokes old Billy indulged in. "Well, he was
full of fun all the time, but winter was when he had
the best of us boys. One of his summer jokes was to
let us fellows load up the single wagon with melons
(and him looking so solemn with his head hanging
down), but no matter how quiet he'd be while we were
piling them in, he seemed to know when we were going
to get the last ones, and while we were picking our
way through the vines, Billy'd start off for home,
and when we'd hurry, he'd hurry, and when we were

about tired out running to catch him, he'd slow up and let us get our breath, then off he'd go again, and blessed if we ever got a ride home behind that horse if he could cheat us. I believe he heard us laughing all the time." "Was he a run-away, then?" "Bless you, no! He couldn't be made to run away, he'd just take them melons home all right. He'd whinner at us when we caught up, just like he enjoyed it." "Did you ever whip him?" "Whip old Billy? Not much! But I was going to tell you his best joke. You see, in winter we go to school, and after school if there was a good deep snow we'd pile onto old Billy and go down to where there was good coasting. How many of us would pile on? Oh, four or five! How could we? Why, he was the longest-built horse you ever saw. Pretty near as long as this wagon-box. By getting onto his neck, six of us could get on. Well, we had to look out for him, for just as sure as he came to a good snow-drift he'd duck his head, and the feller in front would go over, and then before you could say 'scat!' he'd sit down on his hind legs and the rest would slide off backwards; then old Billy'd get up and look at us laughing and scrambling out of the snow." "But didn't any of you ever get hurt?" "No, ma'am! old Billy never dumped us on hard ground; he was just a-joking." "What became of him?" "Died of eating apples. I tell you us boys lost a friend when old Billy died. Have to get out here? Wish you were going further, ma'am. Just let me cramp this wheel so your dress won't get dusty.

All right! Good-by!" The lash cracked, the boys struck up a song, and a cloud of dust haloed their vanishing outlines. I often think of the happy-hearted boys and old Billy.

Guess What.

ONCE there was a flood that surrounded the house where I was living, and it carried drift-wood that lodged in the high branches of trees along bank and across lowlands. After the waters subsided, there were many strange sights; one of them was a kitchen stove in a tree-top, and it remained for eight years that I know of, how much longer I cannot say. One that was on our own place was odd enough.

One morning as the cows were being taken to pasture, the boy discovered a poor little chick helplessly fluttering in the water, and fast drifting down toward the bridge he stood upon. Of course he rescued the chicken and wondered where it came from.

Presently he heard a clucking in the air, and turned slowly around to discover where to locate the sounds. As he held the wet little creature in his handkerchief to dry it, its plaintive cries were heard by the mother, and, to our boy's astonishment, she flew out of a tree-top toward him. Impelled by curiosity, he climbed up, and in a mass of drift-wood some ten feet in diameter, found a brood of fourteen fine chickens. He called loudly, and all ran in haste to see

Biddy's "castle in the air," some fifteen feet above our heads.

They were all brought down in a basket, and were soon in full parade upon level ground, reveling among grass and scouting along the brook's edge for vagrant insects. Biddy showed no disposition to return to her strange lodgings at night, but marched into the fowls' quarter in the barn-yard.

Guess What.

But this lofty retreat was again occupied, and by as strange a tenant, too. The possession of the premises was not even suspected, until one afternoon when I was quietly gathering blackberries (at least the *bees* and I were, and the bees seemed to get the blackest and sweetest ones every time, for they got there

13

earlier than I did), when I heard such pitiful cries, and such a coaxing one too, that I put down my basket and began another kind of search. Up and down the bank I hunted, among grasses and briers. Straightening up for a rest, I found them at last, four frightened kittens cautiously coming down the steep trunk of the tree, in dire dismay of the running water below. We brought a long, wide board, and kitty went up and down on it, bringing one each time to the ground.

It had been a perilous place for both broods, but neither hawks disturbed the one nor mischievous boys the other.

Why should we not learn from these simple examples that the strangest situations are as safe as any if a protecting care is over us?

Obedience.

A COMPARISON BETWEEN A BOY AND A COW.

In a certain place lived a boy whom I will call Johnny. He was about thirteen years old. When a given task was finished, he was quite in the habit of slipping away to the nearest neighbor's to join a companion of his own age, without inquiring first if there was anything else to do, or if his parents were willing to spare him.

He thought that if he was needed he could be called, and did not consider that this looking around for a boy and calling him every time he disappeared was anything of an annoyance. Johnny was not bad; no, no; he was just one of the best boys a mother ever had; it was only lack of understanding on his part.

Promptitude in obeying a summons was another lacking quality in his disposition; he took considerable time before starting, and seldom walked in haste.

His parents kept one cow, who well knew her name,--"Beauty." On a few occasions this cow had been let loose to feed in the orchard, and on one particular day had strayed across the proper line, there being no fence between the two homes.

Johnny's mother happened to look out and saw the two, Johnny chatting with his friend, and Beauty drinking from the neighbor's watering-tub by the well. She called to Johnny, who replied quietly, "All right, in a minute," and immediately relapsed into the interrupted conversation, apparently forgetting altogether that he was wanted. The mother, mortified at the cow's trespass and her son's indifference, called the cow by name, when, to her surprise and great pleasure, Beauty looked up, saw who was calling her, and immediately hastened home. This great comparison between the willing obedience of the dumb creature and the indifference of the one endowed with the gifts of intelligence and speech, caused a hearty laugh from the witnesses of this little incident. I think that Johnny must have felt overwhelmed with regret upon having a cow, by her good example, so gently reproach him.

Daisy and Adeline.

THERE was a little girl twelve years old, and she had a delicate lamb given her, of which she became very fond. When permitted to follow her into the

DAISY AND ADELINE.

house, as sometimes happened, Daisy would stand beside the table where her little mistress was washing dishes, then follow her, step by step, from the table to the cupboard and back, up and down the room, in and out of the house. Daisy never left her side for a moment. One day, for fun, someone said, "See if Daisy would follow you under the bed, Adeline." In the same spirit of amusement, the little girl ran into the bedroom and crept under the bedstead. Daisy scampered after her beloved mistress, but could only get her head and neck under, remaining so, on her knees, until Adeline came out and returned to the other end of the house.

When spring came, the little girl would sometimes climb up on the warm side of the hay-stack and sit there with her knitting or book awhile, and many a one passing by has looked and wondered to see a little girl and white lamb up there. In all Adeline's walks Daisy accompanied her, and many a happy race have they had together. Daisy was so sensible, and when her mistress led her into her warm pen at night and said "good-night" to her, the good little creature always settled down contentedly. The boys could not manage Daisy, she acknowledged but one authority, but to it was truly loyal.

"Good-by, Butterfly."

I TURNED to look. O memory!
Keep fadeless all my life for me
That picture with its lightsome grace
Of floating curls and winsome face,
That backward looked along the fence,
Where, rising higher, floating thence,
A gaudy thing of summer day
Had charmed my boy upon his way.

From flower to flower his steps it led,
Waited a moment, then it fled;
He thought it all in sportive jest,
And joined its course with happy zest,
But, missing me, he passed it by—
"Good-by, butterfly, good-by."

Dear child, may all thy pleasures be
As innocent as this, to thee;
May'st thou with loving heart still heed
The way thy parents' footsteps lead;
Should life's temptations rainbow bright,
Arrest thy steps, allure thy sight,
May'st thou say then, without a sigh,
"Good-by, butterfly, good-by."

Sea=Shells.

ALTHOUGH the children of Utah have manifold
blessings and plenty of healthful play, I often think
of some happy pastimes they never have, as I did
when a child, in my home by the seashore, the Golden
Gate of San Francisco.

There is a wonderful sense of delight in walking
along the seashore and watching the waves running
up to your feet, bringing long wreaths of pretty sea-
weeds, some of bright colors, and laying them upon
the clean, white sand, while they chase back again.
Oh, the sound of the ocean! and oh, the smell of the
sea-grass! And the shells! To gather your hat or
apron full and then find that newer and perhaps prettier ones have been washed ashore; how can anyone
satisfy themselves? You cannot gather them all, and
yet how pretty they all are! You can never tire of
the seaside, for the waves wash out to-morrow the
marks of to-day, and the beach is ever new. Writing
one's name in the sand and then watching the waves
wash it out; how often it has been done! And the
ocean seems talking to you all the time, sometimes
coaxing you to come with bare feet; sometimes changeful like a treacherous heart, so that you dare not trust
it too near; and sometimes so angry that women,
children and even men fear its fury. The Bible speaks
of when the great seas shall "give up their dead."
But, also, the ocean is a great friend; it bears ships of

commerce from one land to another; it brings and
carries the peoples of the earth to visit different countries; and in its waters swarms food for millions of
earth's creatures.   Many wondrous things grow in
its depths that we can handle without fear; beautiful
corals and useful sponges, also shells that are carved
and made into lovely articles for use and adornment;
tortoise shell and mother of pearl, which is used in

THE GOLDEN GATE.

elegant inlaid work.   But most strange and glorious
of all, the Gospel of Jesus Christ has been preached
by a Latter-day Saint to the Gentiles at the bottom
of the sea, in a diving bell.   Can you imagine the
solemnity and grandeur of that place of worship?   In
a diving bell, upon the ocean's floor, with strange
creatures gliding around, and the immensity of dark
water pressing upon them from all sides and above!
Yet the light of the Holy Spirit shone in those cold,

dark depths, and the protecting power of God held back all harm while his children spoke one to another, declaring and listening to his truth. Perhaps this strange circumstance of worship may never again be repeated, until the voice of God's angel calls forth the slumberers of the sea to their resurrection.

Its waters ascend in delicate vapors and temper the hot atmosphere, and by their peculiar properties purify, or carry away, the stale air of many miles in-land. Beautiful, grand and terrible, the ocean is one of God's grandest creations. And those shells! If you pick up one and hold it to your ear, you will find that no matter how far away you have brought it, it has kept in its heart the voice of the sea, and if you will listen it will whisper a song to you. So, dear child, may your heart keep forever in it the echo of the voice far away in the great home you have left for a while.

Says one timid little child who was not born by the sea, "I would rather gather mosses and flowers among the hills." Yes, little one, they are very beautiful also, and many happy hours have I spent in dark woods and warm, bright slopes, gathering them. I am told that many rare ferns grow in our canyons, but it is too far for little feet to go, and so few children can gain that pleasure. There is another enjoyment that some children have, berrying and nutting. But we must remember that we are in what used to be named on the maps, the Great American Desert, and it is so much better now than it was when the Latter-day

Saints came here, that we may hope for nut groves and maple-sugar groves, with blackberries all through them, as in New England, where some of our parents came from. This is the desert that God said should "blossom as the rose" and springs break forth in solitary places. Is it not wonderful to know that we are in the very place He pointed to so many years ago? Is He not smiting the rocks and causing the waters to break forth in waste places?

When we see so much fulfilled, can we doubt that the rest will follow? If His eye is upon this land, it is also watching us. Let us help Him with heart and hand to beautify Zion.

The Indians' Test.

EARLY in the history of the American people, there was a powerful tribe of Indians living close to a white village. The Indians mistrusted the sincerity of the settlers' friendship and showed some signs of this doubt. The white men discovered this and their head men desired a council held to try to arrange some definite terms of peace and security.

The Indians listened to the white men and at last one of them answered for the rest: " We have come at your request and heard your talk. It is near night. If you expect us to have confidence in you, that we may feel safe in your coming and going among us, prove it by letting one of your children spend the

THE INDIANS' TEST.

night with us, and we will bring him to you in the
morning." These words caused a great sensation in
the hearts of the white men, but they knew that a refusal would seal upon them the enmity of the Indians.
One brave man left the room, and in a few moments
returned with his only son. In the presence of all assembled, the father told his son how the safety of the
whole settlement, and perhaps other towns also, depended upon the fulfillment of this obligation. He
told his child that God would watch over him and
bring him back in safety. The dear boy, who was
about six years of age, listened in implicit confidence,
and expressed his willingness to go and not fear the
red men.

As the strange company of warriors filed out of the
settlement, the pretty boy looked back with smiling face
and cried, " Good-night," while hardy men retained
their feelings only until he could no longer discover
their faces. Then, with full hearts, tearful eyes and
trembling tongues, they re-entered the building and
fervently besought God to watch over the precious
hostage lent. Few slept that night; mothers clasped
their babes, and, weeping, prayed. The earliest daylight found watchers gazing upon the distant line of
forest that bordered the plain. At last, figures were
dimly seen approaching, then faster and faster they
came, until the fair face of the beloved child could be
seen. The chief himself led him by the hand to his
parents, and then and there ratified for his people the
compact of peace and defense with the whites. The

child said that they treated him with kindest care,
gave him curious things to please him, and made for
him a bed of softest furs.

How beautiful was this child's obedience and faith,
and of what inestimable value was his courage to
that village! I wish that I could tell you his name,
but have searched in vain for the lost book in which I
read it. How proud must have been every heart
whose life was thus weighed in the mighty balance
against his single one! Perhaps many times that we
know not of, great importance may rest upon the obedience of each one of us, in our path of life as Latter-
day Saints.

Judging Unwisely.

Not many years ago a man rented a store upon a
street appropriately named Market Street. While
very busy getting barrels, boxes and other things inside, he happened to see a boy of eleven years standing by, and called to him, "See here, boy, if you'll
help me to-day, I'll pay you well." The boy looked
at him but made no answer. "Don't you want to
work?" The boy made some sort of gesture, but
remained silent. "Oh! you're some idler, I guess.
Well, if you won't work or even speak, just pass along
about your business." He thought the boy's lounging attitude and continued silence meant disrespect
and defiance, and soon began to feel irritated over it.

JUDGING UNWISELY.

"Some young thief, I guess, watching his chance to steal something and run," thought he. Presently he advanced toward the boy with threatening look, when, to his amazement, the offender performed some peculiar gesture, and strange play of features, as he retreated backward.

"I'll teach you how to make faces and mock me; you've acted the nuisance long enough." And without further delay he raised his hand, when the boy, instead of running off, started, and fell in a heap upon the sidewalk. Several persons hastened to the spot and inquired what was the matter. "Why! that lazy fellow refused work when I offered him pay and hung around even when I ordered him off, and finally made faces and disrespectful gestures at me; so I was going to slap him and he dropped like that. He is not hurt enough to even cry about it." "Sir, that is poor Danny, a deaf mute and cripple, perfectly inoffensive when you know him. We all humor him and let him stay around as long as he pleases, for his eyes are the chief blessings he possesses, and they can't injure anything." When they lifted Danny, they found a bruise upon his forehead, and tears were slowly creeping down his cheeks. He was carried into a store, and one of his friends who understood how to communicate with him, explained the merchant's mistake. You may be sure the man was heartily ashamed, and so anxious to prove his repentance that he did all in his power to relieve poor Danny's adversity and affliction.

Drawing materials, also white blocks of soft wood and patterns, with suitable tools, were furnished, and very often the merchant walked down to the plain house where Danny lived, and often, also, he took the lonely boy for a ride by carriage or railway. A comfortable chair and table with drawers, then by and by a cabinet to hold Danny's works of art, transformed the plain room into an interesting one. The patient mother was very grateful to the new friend, and justly proud of her boy's work; and a pleasant picture they made, sitting in winter beside their glowing fire, with her sewing and Danny busy at his work-table. But for all this good result, the merchant said often: " If I had only known the truth, had not been so hasty in judgment, I might have done as much good without having done any injury."

An Hour with the Aged.

AT a time when I had a nice Sunday-school class, of which I was very fond, there was an aged and very eccentric old lady who was quite particular in the selection of her acquaintances. For some reason of her own, she favored me with her friendship, and it became my custom to start so early to Sunday-school that I could spend an hour with her. Her room was very odd to look at; she had a fancy for putting almost everything into a separate little bag. The hair-brush, coarse and fine combs, were each suspended in a bag just exactly large enough. Even the penholder stuck out of the top of a slender bag that just fitted it. Would you imagine a thimble-bag also? It was a fact. It took me several visits to become accustomed to her oddity. "It was partly on account of the dust, and partly a habit of order," she said. I found out through her kindness of heart that some of these calico bags held a bunch of grapes and an apple each. "I've got grandchildren," she explained.

She also had a Bible so very old that the pages were yellow, and it was so large it was awkward to hold. Many a pleasant talk we had, she explaining to me passages that were obscure. How I loved to read the writings of Esdras in the Apocrypha, and how odd were some of the names in the old Bible! Such old-fashioned ear-rings as she wore, too. One day I asked her if she had not had them a long time, for my mother had, hidden safely away, a pair something like them that grandpa gave her for her fifth birthday, when he came home with his ship. Said she, "My husband put these in my ears forty years ago on our wedding-day, and I want them buried with me."

It so happened that her wish was fulfilled that same summer, and it was my mournful pleasure to attend her last hours and moments in this life.

Dear children, it is a sacred pleasure to realize that you have lightened a few hours of the aged and lonely who have been withdrawn from the sunshine and cheerfulness of outdoor existence. If it is your privi-

14

lege to do so, let your ministrations help them to forget a portion of their sorrow and pain, and perhaps they may bear a kind word for you to the higher and better world.

An Hour with the Lowly.

WHEN about twelve years of age, I attended a day-school nearly a mile from home. The walk was a pleasant one, bordered with luxuriant fields, and wild flowers grew in abundance by the way. Such a merry group were we, ofttimes singing all together some favorite song.

Upon our way home I sometimes stopped at the door of a humble dwelling, inhabited by Aunt Harriet, a colored woman, to get a cool drink. One afternoon she very respectfully asked if I would read aloud to her a hymn; she had heard it sung and had learned part, and although she had bought a handsomely-bound hymn-book, she could not read it. "I bought the best binding to show my respect for the insides, honey, and because I like to have it in the house along with the Bible. I know I've got the good Lord's words with me, whether I can read it or not; and if I can get someone to read to me once in a while, I'll get the whole good of it by and by." So I would sit in the easy-chair, and read a chapter or a hymn to the good woman, who would fan away the flies as I read.

Sometimes we would sing the hymn together, to make sure she had the words right. Once in a while Aunt Harriet would sing for me a mournful plantation melody, and I appreciated it very much. I rejoiced with her that she was in a "free State," after she had told me of the sorrowful separation she had suffered in her native State. "I had one baby, honey, and they sold him out of my arms when he learned to dance so pretty." I told her how Harriet Beecher Stowe had written "Uncle Tom's Cabin," and how through it the Northern people felt about slavery. At last I brought it to her house, and read a few pages to her every night until it was finished. "Honey, it's next to the Bible," she would say; and, oh, how many blessings the author had from the lips of Aunt Harriet! If I was behind the others on the way home, I lost nothing by it; my heart was always happier, and did not Aunt Harriet always put into my hand a cake or a large piece of the nicest pie to eat on the way home? Now and then I think of the pretty little adobe house so neat and clean, the garden glowing with hundreds of flowers, and all so comfortable without and within. Uncle Grief was a real gentleman at heart, and the couple were respected by all who knew them. Father had Southern ideas, and my mother the opposite, but they both approved of my visits to the little cabin.

The Rich and the Poor: Currant Picking.

WHEN the long, cold winter has passed, the wet, variable spring weather also, and the gardens are all planted, there comes a halting-time between the end of last year's income and the beginning of the new season's sales. Among the farmers the very first things raised must be sold for those things most needed. If the children want to earn a little pocket-money, they do not expect to get it out of the asparagus and pieplant, lettice or radishes; no, these must buy groceries, perhaps shoes; but the children all over Utah can gather, in June, currants and sell them and have the money for their own.

The currants of Utah are, to the children who will gather them, like "the cranberries on the moor," and other wild berries which the children of many countries gather and sell. And how pretty these currant hedges are—the first to show the green leaves and the first to bloom in the spring! And when the pioneers came here, they must have been very glad to find them, for wild berries are not common here as in other States and Territories. Was not this once " the great American desert"? Yes, though it does not look so now.

I did not think of currants as an income, until I knew how some little girls stood in the sun for hours picking the currants and then took them to town to

sell, offering them to a lady who was noted for her
luxurious living and public charities. These children,
by two days' incessant labor at a distance from home,
going and returning over glistening stubble-fields and
dusty road, had, by a close calculation, earned enough
to buy them each a much-desired straw hat to wear
to Sunday-school instead of their winter ones. The
lady had a guest, and the two repaired to the dining-
room to look at the fruit the little girls had brought.
"I think eight cents a quart rather high," said the
lady. "Dear me!" added her friend, "these things
grow almost wild everywhere; the children have
nothing to do but to pick them. I should think five
cents enough."

The little girls, warm with the long, jolting ride,
looked at the ladies in their elegant attire, surrounded
by rich furniture, and wondered how they could con-
descend to quibble over such a small sum. Disheart-
ened, they went to several other places, and at each
refusal felt more abashed, and at last halted, undecided
whether to try even once more. All the bright hopes
were dull now; the sun was warm; they were foot-
weary, and they must not keep the kind neighbor
waiting too long; they were hungry, too. The great
city did not look to them as they had expected. Everything seemed in such a rush, everybody for themselves,
so indifferent, almost heartless. How nice home was!
In such meditative mood they reached another gate,
and before either had time to ask, "Shall we go in
here?" a kind voice inquired, "My dears, have you

something to sell?" They looked at the speaker and
felt an instant relief, for her face was gentle and sympathetic, as though she could see their timidity and
weariness. "Yes, ma'am, Utah currants," answered
Annie, the elder sister. "Come in out of the sun. I'll
look at them." This they were very glad to do, and
when they stepped upon the wide and long porch, all
screened in with vines, a canary trilled out a sort of
welcome from his cage high up in the cool shadows.
A cat with her kitten lay curled up in an arm-chair
just inside the hall, and how quiet, and peaceful, and
sweet everything looked! They passed into a cool
dining-room, where dinner was just over but not removed. "You look very warm and tired, my dears,
and perhaps you have not yet had your dinners; if
not, sit down and have something while we talk about
this fruit." Noticing their hesitation, she gently drew
them to the table and drew several dishes of food before them, then opened their baskets. By gentle
questions the lady learned all their story, of the distance from town, the hours in the hot sun, the ride to
town with the good neighbor, and then the many dis-
appointments. As the recital drew near the end, how
their faces changed expression as they looked in her
friendly face!

"You are deserving of praise for your industry and
perseverance, and I will take these twelve quarts of
you, and whatever else you bring to town come to me
first and I will give you my custom, whether it be
fruit, or butter and eggs, if they are as nice as these."

The lady asked them many questions, and found that they had improved their scanty advantages, being able to tell her in an interesting manner what they had learned. When they rose to go, how different were their feelings compared with their calls at other houses! They had met a lady indeed, though not a rich one, and had experienced feelings of gratitude and pleasure instead of mortification and shame in their honest efforts.

You may be sure that after that day their friend was served with the earliest and best products from the little farm, with all punctuality, and when the winter school opened, two certain little girls appeared at the school-house door the very first morning, comfortably attired and equipped with well-filled satchels, cheerful faces and eager minds ready for the winter campaign of learning.

I do not think that the rich realize, generally, how sensitive may be the feeling of those who have to earn their means in the small ways of life.

Yet in the days of our Saviour, he asked, "Are not two Sparrows sold for a farthing?" How few now earn their living in as small a way as that, or their bread by gleaning, and yet how beautiful, though centuries old, is the story of the life, how exalted the character, of Ruth, the gleaner!

Frosted Cake and the Moss Rose Set.

IT was near Christmas-time, and pretty Francelle Cummings came in from shopping, her cheeks glowing and eyes sparkling with exhilaration, for had not her father given her just as much pocket-money as she had asked him for that morning? Enough to satisfy her "for a beginning," she said; and how many lovely things she had brought home.

'I stopped to see what Cousin Ella was going to get, and what do you think she was doing?" "Something sensible, I have no doubt," replied the mother. "Well, I don't know; some persons have such extraordinary ideas. I suppose she thought it was sensible. She was making pies and cakes, herself, to donate to the poor for Christmas (I don't believe she'll make one of her friends a present); and what do you really think—she was making fruit-cakes and sponge-cakes and frosting them! Just as though plain cake wasn't good enough for folks who never have any of their own! I was so surprised, I came away without comment, for I had counted on her going shopping with me. And—I came near forgetting—the nicest pair of cakes was for Mrs. Whitney."

Francelle looked quite relieved now, and, after trailing around before the glass, sat down and glanced from her mother to her aunt to note the effect of her statement.

FROSTED CAKE AND THE MOSS ROSE SET.

Now this aunt had only lately come from a long distance to visit them during the winter, having been parted from her only brother, Francelle's father, for many years.

"Francelle, dear, how much do you suppose that Ella's Christmas gifts to the poor will cost?" "Oh, I don't know, mother; the eatables might amount to three or four dollars; of course it's not the expense, it's the idea. Then I wouldn't wonder if she has some flannels and other missionary articles to go along with the rest that might make eight or ten dollars more. I don't really know, of course; but that's her style."

"Will it offend, if I ask what your Christmas gifts to friends will probably cost you?" "Certainly not, auntie; I've bought a ring for ma, something for you, a lovely lace handkerchief for Cousin Annie; a box of gloves, a set of furs, a ball dress, with suitable belongings to match—I guess that's all to-day; I suppose seventy-five dollars will be the sum; I sent the bill for part of it to pa." "Thank you, dear. I feel like telling you a little Christmas story, if you like." Francelle, who at first feared just a little that auntie was not in accord with her, now that nothing serious had been said by way of reproof (ma was always indulgent), expressed her desire to listen; for Francelle was insatiate in her love of something new and interesting."

"Many years ago there lived in New York a good old-fashioned man and wife, who had two daughters. Occasionally there came to visit the family a very wealthy gentleman, a business acquaintance of the old

merchant. The family lived in the suburbs, just where
gardens and hedged lanes began, a pleasant retreat
after the business cares of the day.

"The daughters had considered the gentleman as
their parents' visitor, being too modest to think that
their attractions had anything to do with his calls;
nor indeed were they mistaken. So it was quite natural that, after having spent some time in the parlor,
one of the young ladies excused herself and retired.
Perhaps half an hour later she reappeared, and remarked to her parents that she was going out for a
short walk. It happened, quite unintentionally, that
the gentleman had just risen to take his leave, and he
asked permission to accompany her along the lane as
far as the main road. Josephine looked toward her
parents, who replied, ' Certainly,' and the pair pro·
ceeded from the house, Josephine to walk a few
blocks, the gentleman to return to the heart of the
great city.

"Josephine wore that evening a light, satin-finished
French calico, something like our present sateens, of
ivory-tinted groundwork, with dainty moss rose buds
upon it. The waist was made surplice fashion, that
is, with fine folds diagonally across from shoulder to
belt, the mutton-leg sleeves, then in vogue, delicate
lace coming down to a point in the neck, scant skirt,
short enough to reveal silk hose and neat slippers.
A fine white Leghorn hat with brim tied down gypsy
fashion by pale ribbons, and right above her jet-black,
waving hair, a blush rose. Lace gloves completed the

costume. Her companion was a gentleman of careful breeding, and not the suggestion of a compliment passed his lips. At the end of the lane he asked, ' If I receive your father's permission, may I hope to take a walk with you one week from to-night?' Josephine, knowing her parents' good opinion of the gentleman, assented, not that she regarded him with any new interest. He added, ' Please wear this dress.' Josephine returned home before lamp-light, and related the request made at the termination of the short walk together. Her father replied: ' Mr. Waldron is a gentleman of fine qualities, and you have my sanction in receiving his addresses, if congenial to your own feelings.' Her mother added: ' Mr. Waldron is, in rare instances, eccentric; but he does you much honor by his attention, which would be appreciated by many another.'

"Josephine had never thought of any person as a suitor, and thought little of the matter during the week, except his odd request that she should wear that same dress.

"Accordingly, when he called again, and, after spending a couple of hours as formerly, turned to Josephine and asked, ' Shall we walk as far as the church?' she replied and left the room, returning in a brief time attired as the week before, and they took their departure. After half an hour's walk they stood before a large edifice, a Lutheran Church, and went in. After the evening service, he waited while the throng passed out, then, turning to the lovely girl, said:—

"'Josephine, when I looked at you one week ago in that costume, I made up my mind to try and win you before another man should be charmed like myself and snatch you away from me. Your father has consented to our union, and I desire to go forth from this church this evening with you as my wife. The minister is waiting.' Like one bewildered and fascinated, Josephine bowed assent, and they went up the aisle, when, in the presence of a few whom the minister had asked to wait, they were married.

"They passed forth from the building and walked for some distance, Josephine taking no notice of the direction, when Mr. Waldron stopped at a gate. Within were lawn, elegant shrubbery and flowers, and a pretty white cottage. Mr. Waldron opened the door and entered. At the left hand they entered a parlor. Imagine Josephine's surprise to see the room's furniture upholstered in ivory white and gold with moss roses. 'Let us go upstairs.' The bedroom was a match for the parlor below. 'Let us go into the dining-room.' To her surprise, a table for two was in waiting, and the same pretty thought was there represented again. 'I have devoted this week to what you see; much of it has been made to my order. Does it please you?' 'Yes, but it is all so sudden, so like a fairy tale, I can hardly realize.' 'When this little home grows dull for you, a grander one shall be yours, a marble mansion, when you desire it.' Before Josephine's trembling lips could answer, he touched a bell and a woman entered. They were made known to each other. The housekeeper bowed and wished her mistress many happy years. Supper was brought in, and after this was over, he led the wondering Josephine back to the parlor. He seated himself at the piano and rendered such rare music as Josephine had never dreamed.

"'Come, let us go back to your father and mother, and to-morrow I will bring them with you to see our home.' So saying, they went into the street and back to the dear old home. 'Let me tell you where we have been,' said he. The parents were surprised, surely, but when he bade them good-night, leaving the lovely Josephine in their care, all were satisfied. The morning brought him, with carriages, and a happy party went to the pretty cottage.

"Ten years Mr. Waldron and his wife lived there, then, as he had said on that wedding-night, they moved into an elegant marble mansion. In that abode of luxury, after a few years, Josephine heard of Mormonism, and went to listen to the prophet Joseph, himself. Josephine feared to tell her husband, for she had heard his scornful mention of the new sect. Years of faith and prayer and suspense passed by, as she dared not speak to him of the man he called an 'impostor,' and the religion he spoke of as a 'fraud.' At last the storm broke, and Josephine had to choose between wealth in the world or poverty among the Saints. Husband and children in one scale, the people of God in the other. This is the woman for whom your cousin Ella, in blissful ignorance, has made her nicest cakes, and 'frosted them,' too. I sought her out when I came here, for we were friends in girlhood."

Francelle burst into tears, and it took auntie's own kind words to prove to her that she was not really a heartless, selfish girl, and she listened with pathetic deference while auntie concluded:—

"Remember, dear girl, that poor people may have had at one time the same luxuries that you have, perhaps more. If so, they must miss these things as almost the necessities of life. If not, the bounty of the rich will surely be appreciated by them." "Auntie, you called him Mr. Waldron?" "So I did. Don't you see the reason?"

This story is from life, and much more might be told of elders aided, families provided for and emigrated by the noble, self-sacrificing Josephine. She still lives among us, and though of "silver and gold" she has none now to impart, her spirit charms and inspires love and reverence.

Respect for the Aged.

SOME young girls on their way to Sunday-school cast many humorous glances and subdued tittering toward one of their own age who was walking quietly along beside a venerable man, one who had helped "build up the country." It was observed by the pair, but they cared little for it, only the thoughtless girls did themselves an injustice. It was inappropriate conduct on any day, but upon the Lord's day it seemed even more unbecoming. In former times church-going persons went to their worship reverently, and, reaching the house of God, entered with the utmost respect. When seated, they did not twist around in their seats to gaze at some new-comer; perfect attention was given to the sermon, and it was the theme at home in the evening.

Clothing, however rich or poor, need not be scanned or criticised; when you and I came upon this earth, we were treated equally in that respect. But to return to the subject. The gray-haired man was a Sunday-school teacher, and had taken the pains to invite some new residents to attend meetings and Sunday-school, and, seeing the timidity of the young lady, invited her to walk with him. This was true kindness and courtesy on his part. I know he was once taken a little by surprise when a young person, meeting him, bowed and quietly said, "Good-afternoon." Said he in relating the incident, "I thought a good deal of that bit of politeness, for young folks don't notice me on the street, they pass right along." If, in meeting a person upon the street, you slightly bow, or lift the hat, it does not mean an invitation to form an acquaintance. It always looks well for one who is well dressed to render a slight inclination of the head if meeting another less favored of fortune. The poor and the laboring classes already feel the comparison between their and your circumstances keenly enough without any display of conscious superiority or ill-bred pride.

I know of a tired little boy who, coming from his long day's work, was mortified to meet a nicely-dressed young lady, but said he that night at home, "She spoke just as politely to me as if I had been Brother Brigham, and she's the nicest and best woman in the world, and I'm going to be as near like her as I can." Some years later he was her escort through a wild portion of country, and he seemed to take delight in bestowing every attention to her and her little children. If she had turned up her nose or giggled at him, do you suppose he could have felt as well toward her?

The lounger, the vagabond and the wicked are easily recognized, and have no claim to our notice, but among strangers many we meet are our equals and some our superiors. Let me relate an incident which occurred perhaps twelve years since, in Salt Lake City, as told to me by the young man, who is now a very prominent and beloved gentleman, whom you all know. "I was upon the sidewalk and approaching the crossing. I was in great haste, and as I neared the plank an aged man was in advance of me. I hastily took a few long steps, intending to get there ahead of him. Another step and I would have accomplished it, but, as I brushed close to him, he turned, saw my eagerness, and politely lifted his hat, stepping aside for me to pass. My momentum was such that I could not stop before I had one foot on the plank, but there I paused, transfixed with shame, a very tableau of precipitate haste and rudeness! We gazed in each other's eyes until he kindly extended his hand in

15

acknowledgment of my distressed apologies, which I
knew by his gracious smile and adieu he understood.
I could not speak his language, but I learned then and
there a lesson from him that I have never forgotten."

RESPECT TO OTHERS.

There is another thing I would like to mention,
which is, speaking of others with too great familiarity.
Shall we not speak of our friend as Brother Joseph Hall
instead of Jo Hall, especially as the gentleman is
one of your Ward Teachers? Remember him as an
officer in the church of which you are a member.
Strive to emulate the calling and mission of the
Teachers, *guardians of peace and guides to truth.*
Well, if you think "that's as good as a motto," write
it on your book-mark, for it is true. The Teachers
have your welfare more closely in view than even
your Bishop. Their frequent visits have given them
an insight into your heart; they know your life and
circumstances. In sickness they are to be depended
upon for consolation and spiritual aid; you can go to
them for counsel, for advice in worldly matters, and if
you are in sorrow you can confide in them. You may
think their office a small one, but I can tell you the
Teachers of the Ward are like the index to the book;
go to them for what you want to find. Boys, you can
never become a Bishop, President of a Stake, or at-
tain to any other high calling until you have qualified
yourselves as Teachers. Therefore, honor them and
strive to win and keep their confidence.

The Rover's Native Tongue.

HE was a tall, rough-bearded man,
　Had roamed o'er sea and plain,
And seemed apart from other's lives,
　Like one who sought in vain
To win the hope for which he sought,
　Or as he little cared
For friend or love or passing joys,
　Or perils he had shared.

Yet once, as light beams through a cloud,
　Some memory seemed to wake,
And many a tale of life he told,
　Like dreams that glow and break
In restless sleep; and names slipped in
　From many a foreign land.
Ah, his had been a rover's life,
　Linked with some Corsair band!

"The tongues of many lands you've learned;
　Now, when you are alone,
And thinking only to yourself,
　Which language seems your own?"
"Lady, wherein I chance to be
　That country's is my own,
To speak or think, to sing or read,
　With others or alone.

"But oh! though wanderer from home
　Since when my years were young,
In dreams, their scenes and all my thoughts
　Are in my native tongue;

For, deep adown this rover's heart,
    Like treasures buried deep,
The words learned from his mother's lips
    Uncovered glow in sleep.

" Like lamps or stars at night they shine,
    O'er land or water's foam,
In solitude they wake my heart
    And fondly call me home."
Sing on, O mothers, to your babes,
    Nor count the moments loss,
Thy hymns and prayers and tender words
    Shall span the world across.

Bees, Their Habits and What They Did.

THERE was a great commotion in a certain hive of
bees, for it had been announced that one of the brood
cells was being enlarged and fitted up appropriately
for the occupancy of a royal infant, a future queen-
bee.

There was a great hurrying to and fro, large numbers were sent out to bring in an increased supply of
pollen for bee bread and wax, while the honey gatherers had special orders for an unlimited quantity of
sweets, well, as much as the hive would hold. The
drones were ordered to stand out of the way of the
committees and workers, as well as to keep a respect-

ful distance from the attendants of the royal infant and
her august mother, the queen. None of these subjects ever turn their backs upon the queen, but advance and retire with the utmost deference and skill.
There are no upstarts in bee society, they are all properly reared from birth.

While a number of professional excellence were re-
citing or singing to her majesty. still others sought to
conceal from her serenity the fact of the oppressive
heat outside, by a thoughtful use of their wings as
fans, thus creating a circulation of air delicately perfumed by the merest suggestions of the most exquisite
flora adorning an expansive and charming landscape.
Neither overwhelmed nor oppressed by these refined
attentions, the reflective faculties of her majesty wandered in delicious fancy over realms of nature boun-
teous in resources and rapturous to the eye; but, having the interests of her well-ordered kingdom and
loyal subjects at heart, she stifled the desire which the
vision impelled, by this noble and exquisite self-sacrificing sentiment. "Not yet; I must not desert my
royal duties at this important time for my personal
gratification." Revealing no sign of this mental conflict and victory over self, the queen directed her
thoughts toward subjects of present importance, and
deliberated upon the provisions necessary for the dignity and station of the royal infant, and in a short time
the matter was decided in her own mind and set aside
until the time for action should arrive. As the authority of a queen-bee is absolute, and no prime

ministers or parliaments presume to arrogate to themselves superior wisdom and present their advice, and
her majesty never asks any, but proceeds always according to the original constitution framed by the
Grand Organizer of the Bee Kingdom (which has never
had any amendments appended to it), there was no
cause for any anxiety or further consideration, so she
graciously listened to the soft harmony of voices rising from the populace of contented spirits and willing
hands, and her mind and heart felt to ask for nothing
further at the disposal of nature, but relapsed into
blissful ease, unlike many sordid and avaricious mon-
archs, whose reflections in times of peace are upon
conquest and plunder.

The pollen gatherers returned, and their work was
assigned them, some to the refectory, while others,
the wax-makers, repaired to their own department.
In less than a minute, nearly one hundred of these
ran up to a cross at the top, and, catching hold with
their foreclaws, swung off as though practicing a
trapeze performance. Quicker than I can tell you,
another set followed, and, catching onto the hind legs,
dangling down, called out to the rest to come along.
This was repeated until a perfect curtain, all sparkling
with dazzling eyes, quivering wings and a background
of gold and polished black stripes, shaded with velvety
brown, hung before your astonished eyes. "Do your
legs ache?" called out the bees below, and the brave
little fellows above answered back, "We can stand it;
stick to your work." And so they did, until the wax

came out in rings around their bodies. Then other workers hurried to them and began pulling off the wax and tucking it in pockets in their hind legs, until it rounded out and no more would hold on. As fast as the wax-makers were relieved of their manufactures, they let go of those above and hurried away, to their dinners, I suppose. The little fellows with the wax in their pockets ran around to where the masons were at work gauging and measuring off the six-sided cells for honey storage, bee bread, and brood apartments. You ought to have seen them claw out a clawful of sweet, clean wax, put it in place, and pat it to just the right angle and thickness, a little thicker up and down the corners, a little thinner in the center of the walls, until almost like paper and clear enough for light to show through it, but strong enough to hold a hundred times its weight in honey, I do believe. They run up these cells very fast, and their work is so clean, no chips and dust do these carpenters leave, and so tempting to the eye that you would want to have a chew of it, if you are like every girl and boy I ever knew.

The very minute the cells were ready, along came the honey bringers and poured in the delicate nectar. "Here!" called out an expert in sampling honey, "this has been made from sage blossoms; it is very strong. What is to be done with it?" One of the "Committee on Arrangements" stepped forward, and, with a low bow, replied: "It will be the very finest of medicated sage honey, for cases of canker, and as there is but one known range of country where it can be procured, we have the advantage of the supply." "Very well," replied the sampler, "but the demand for canker medicine is not very great; what is this fiery lot?" "That was brought from the ranges and plains of wild mustard blossoms, and might be used in the manufacture of piccalilli, of which our masters are so fond." "The supply is quite sufficient for the piccalilli market of the entire season; we want no more of it. But this is fine indeed, although rather dark in color, and the flavor is new to me." "This, sir, is from the earliest fruits, chiefly the native berries; and this, from field and orchard blossoms, combining all their delicate flavors," answered the bee respectfully. The sampler marked the latter A No. 1, and the fruit-culled sample, B No. 2, then ordered them deposited in the whitest of the new-made comb, and covers capped on, marked with their private, undiscoverable and inimitable trade-mark.

Just as this order had been delivered, an outcry was raised that an intruder, a moth, the deadly enemy of the bee tribe, had overpowered the guard and rushed in already, working his way to the brood department, with the dastardly purpose of slaying first the young, and then, taking advantage of the distracted state of the adult population in their bereavement, to let in his accomplices without. In an instant the order was given to head him off and get him into a corner. As soon as this was accomplished, a call was made for masons and plasterers, and the judge ordered a solid wall

built across the angle, and high enough to roof it over
and seal it hermetically tight.   The moth tried to offer
some compromise, but his voice was drowned by a
tumult of outcries that their laws were antediluvian
and irrevocable, and, in the case of moths, there could
be heard no appeal or arbitration.   The sentence was
imprisonment until death.   Neither would the remains be remanded to relatives or friends after death.
His own had looked their last upon him when they
sent him forth as a spy and plunderer.   Thus the
enemy outside, who awaited a signal from their vent-
urous comrade, were disappointed, for their eyes never
again rested upon him.   So might it be with all trai-
tors.

Order and activity were now resumed, and after the
roll was called, report was made of those who had
been killed by kingbirds while on their trip, and of
others snapped up by toads while resting a moment
on the step of the hive on their return.   The attendants upon her majesty the infant princess, and the
rest of the youthful colony, also the treasurer, reported the condition of their respective charges.   A
consultation was also held upon the matter of some
fifty pounds of honey that had been taken from the
hive the day before and sold, the exact pantry closet
where it was now hidden having been discovered by
a scouting bee.   It was resolved to recover the
honey on the following day.

.   .   .   .

Early next morning the lady of a certain house

decided to take a ride for her health, and breakfast
with her sister. The visit lasted all day, and when
they returned at night she said to her husband, "We
will just have a cup of tea with bread and butter, and
some of that fresh honey, instead of cooking supper."
Accordingly, after the table was otherwise ready, she
took a beautiful glass dish and silver knife and proceeded to the inner closet. Imagine her surprise
when she saw only the pure white honey-comb. It
was certainly a mystery, for how could anyone steal
honey out of a locked room and without taking the
comb. She thought about fairies' work, although she
did not believe in such fantastical creatures. Upon
close examination, a very little honey was left, but without taking it, the lady went back to the dining-room
with something else. It could not be comprehended
that night, but they found out the secret next morning.

When she opened the dining-room door, she heard a
buzzing, and, following the sound, went into the pantry
and found bees flying in and out through the slatted
window. The lady watched them settle upon the
honey, then fly away. She called her husband, and
he laughed at the wise little creatures. "Well," said
she, "I paid Mrs. James for that honey, and her bees
have stolen it back, but I'll have her come over and
see for herself, after breakfast." When the top of the
kitchen stove was opened, the inside was swarming
with bees. They soon flew outdoors when a smoke
was made and brandished around them, and Mr.

Blake proceeded to kindle the fire for his wife, but, strangely enough, it would not draw. Clouds of smoke puffed out of the stove, but very little out of the pipe.

"A hundred years or so ago, they would have called this witchcraft," said Mr. Blake, smiling, "but I'll simply take the pipe down. Some idle boy may have been playing us a trick while we were gone, though I can't imagine who;" and he lifted the pipe carefully so as not to drop soot on the floor before taking it outdoors. "Goodness! what is that? I can't see for the smoke," he exclaimed, and then rushed out of the house, forgetful of soot or clean floor. In a minute or less the room was full of buzzing bees, all darting for the door to get fresh air. Who had ever heard of such a thing before? The bees had been determined to get into the house after the honey, and some had gone down the stove pipe while others went in at the window.

Mrs. James came over and saw how it was, and cheerfully restored the amount of honey carried away by her bees. (Now, this is a true circumstance, for I saw the identical empty honey-comb, and also the lady's kitchen before the stove pipe was replaced.) " I should think, Mrs. James, that your bees might be taught to come in to the table and eat; they seem very intelligent," said Mr. Blake good-humoredly, and to his enlightenment the lady replied: "Although I have never invited them to eat at my table, I have, in times of scarcity of bee forage in the early spring (especially

as I had taken more honey from them in the fall than
I should have done), prepared several articles of food
for them, and set it conveniently on a bench in front of
their hives; and they very appreciatively accepted it."
Mr. Blake smiled in surprise, and inquired what kind
of food. "Sometimes I would dilute syrup or sugar
with water, at other times a plate of very nice preserves. Trying to approach the substitute for pollen,
I offered them fine corn-meal, which they also ate,
and it was my habit to kill once a week a tender
young chicken, prepare it as neatly as for my own
cooking, and then boil it tender, and set it on a clean
plate before them. They generally ate most of the
meat. I think they would not have cared for the meal
or meat if they could have found sufficient of their
natural food, but at any rate my bees lived through
the season of scarcity, without any injury to their
health, I think, for they all cast off their swarms as
usual. But I would never again rob them so closely
in the fall; they have a right to their own provisions
sufficient for the season."

. . . .

Now while all this excitement was going on, and
after the bees reported the recovery of the honey, affairs had not been at a stand-still in the hive. It was
apparent to every member of the hive that the royal
infant was growing so fast (I should have said the
princess) that her interests as a future sovereign demanded official attention; for what is sovereignty
without subjects and a kingdom, and the chief persons

in her majesty's suite awaited with intense yet defer-
ential anxiety the mention of the matter by the queen,
knowing full well that not even the most devoted of
her subjects could understand the subject better, or
feel it more deeply at heart, than her own maternal
promptings and judgment could dictate. So, while
their minds were at this tension, the summons came,
and with all promptness was responded to. The royal
mother, in august council assembled, declared her intention of abdicating in favor of her daughter, prefer-
ring to situate her among subjects already devoted to
her, and called upon a few of her faithful ones to go with
her to settle some new place.   If a few of the younger
colonists felt an ardent desire for exploration, and the
laborious duties of establishing a new kingdom in a
new country, a few volunteers had the privilege. This
announcement threw the whole populace into excitement, but there were wise heads enough to steady
everything, and organize both the new young government at home and the great expedition. The queen
announced that with an escort she would take a short
trip through the air, and overlook the prospect. Accordingly she sent out a weather-wise scout to ascertain if the sky was propitious. The report being
favorable, the queen took a brief trip *incognito*, and
returned well satisfied with her investigations.   As
she re-entered the hive, a loud acclaim made known to
her that the royal daughter was addressing her devoted attendants. The queen, then, charging such of
her subjects as should remain, to preserve their estab-

lished customs of union, order, industry, frugality, and loyalty, also all their laws of government, arts, and sciences, as handed down to them by their ancestors, surrounded by a loyal throng of followers and defenders, each with his own keen sword, bade them farewell, with her blessing, and took her course forth upon her memorable expedition in search of a new place to found a kingdom. Giving orders to her reconnoitering advance guard, the queen resigned herself to zealous enjoyment of the journey.

A certain aged tree, with a large cavity, first discovered and prospected in by a woodpecker, afterwards occupied by a hermit owl, and later by squirrels, was designated as the chosen spot. Arriving there in due time, after a pleasant journey over a lovely landscape, the queen alighted for an extended observation of the scene. Crops in succession, and others of perennial growth, promised permanent harvests.

While enjoying and remarking upon these advantages, the air seemed to darken a little, as though portending a storm, and the bees clustered around her majesty to shut off any coolness. An alarming sight now presented itself, an old farmer scanning the sky, and holding a tin pan in his hand, while his wife was hastily brushing out an old hive. With all possible haste the queen led her subjects into the cavity in the great tree. In a short time it was discovered that some drones had followed the expedition, possibly in search of lucrative positions or royal favor, for idlers are ever sordid and unprincipled, whether insect or

human. These obnoxious parasites of the new kingdom were therefore treated to a mandate just issued,—
to leave the society of their fellow-creatures. Indulg-
ing in the vain hope of toleration, they lingered, loth
to make any effort to maintain themselves, when
prompt justice was meted out to them. Seized upon
at either side, they were hurried forward to the en-
trance, and there reproached in stern tones for the de-
pravity of their characters, in eating the bread of the
laborer, and not even bearing a sword to draw in defense of their sovereign. Their great, burly bodies and
glossy coats were ridiculed, their empty pockets
pointed to, and at last, time being too precious to
waste further upon them, they were thus stigmatized:
"As your wings are never used upon errands of diligence, we take them from you," and, suiting the action
to the word, they sawed them off, and pushed the
drones over the edge, from whence they fell to the
ground. Piratical and gormandizing reptiles seized
upon them, and their lamentations were soon lost in
deep holes or tangled grass.

The sky soon darkened, thunder pealed, lightnings
flashed, and, for a while, the situation was appalling;
for as yet there were no supplies, excepting that some
member had brought along a day's rations, and this was
made to go all around. But the storm was only a
thunder-shower, and that night the moon and stars
shone out clearly, and all was sweet and still. Next
morning before her majesty awoke, a large proportion
of her subjects set out with energy, and by diligent

labor soon returned with sufficient material for the manufacture of comb and honey. Work progressed rapidly, and in one month they were quite well off, and it was only the middle of June. Then what? Let me tell you. You remember about the old farmer?

Having once got the idea in his head that bees were around, he kept a lookout, and at last traced them from his clover-field right home to their tree. How he laughed and hurried home, then hastened back with ax, pails, and hive. "Found a bee gum," said he, and the family followed him with all delight and earnestness. It was just a little cloudy that day, so most of the bees were around home, for it is considered unwise among bees to go abroad in doubtful weather, for thunder has a disastrous effect upon their systems. As they anxiously watched the weather indications, they observed that field-mice and angleworms were throwing up fresh dirt, and the birds flew in flocks, with great uneasiness and apparent dissatisfaction. Another thing that they observed was worse than a thunder-storm, the veritable old farmer, coming with his family and all those things. The bees kept very quiet, but he came right up to the tree, and squinted cautiously around.

"I'm certain this is the tree, though I don't see any bees to-day; just climb up and listen at that hole, will you, John?" John did not ascend with as much readiness as though he were hunting nuts or grapes, but cautiously neared the hollow and listened. "Yes, father," and John came down as quickly as he could.

Then something like a clap of thunder shook the

tree, and every bee was stunned a moment, but recovered and rushed out to defend their queen and castle. A dreadful smoke hid the enemy from sight and confused the bees. Again and again the sharp ax shook the tree. Her majesty inquired the nature of these shocks, and before her faithful subjects could frame so heart-rending an explanation, she comprehended from their distress the situation, and exclaimed that there was no hope of escape. Presently there was an outcry that the honey was pouring over everything and drowning hundreds of her subjects. A strange creaking sound and a difficulty in keeping right side up was followed by a tremendous jar! The tree was prostrate upon the ground, and the farmer's ax laid the trunk wide open. While his family secured the pailfuls of honey, the farmer transferred the masses of bees to the hive, and covered it to begin his homeward march. Amidst all this confusion and distress, the voice of the queen was heard, and produced a magical effect: "We are spared to each other, and let us begin anew with that fortitude which belongs to our race, and replenish our stores and increase our numbers. At a favorable opportunity, we will again seek a location far removed from the evil influences of tyranny and usurpation." Her majesty's devoted people immediately rallied around her with assurances of devotion and obedience, and as soon as they were thoroughly established in their enforced quarters, resumed their labors on the following day with a patience and zeal worthy of their illustrious progenitors, the royal bees of the house of King Solomon.

16

How a Boy Went Fishing.

On the morning of Decoration-day, Harry declined attending the celebration with the family, saying that he preferred to go fishing, "lots of other fellows were going." So Harry gathered up his fishing outfit, his gun, dinner pail, matches, and an umbrella for sultry sun or summer shower, and set them outside the door while he hunted for a few angleworms.

The parents bade him good-by, to take care of himself, and not go too far up the canyon, for the walk home after pleasure is over is always a longer one than that of going.

When the parents and two youngest ones returned from the celebration that afternoon, the good house-keeper had a nice, plain dinner ready; the two children left in her care were asleep after their dinner, and the house seemed peaceful and cool after the long ride and exercises in the open air.

Just before lamp-light, Harry came home, all his trim outfit looking very dusty and out of order; the umbrella was broken, the dinner pail dented and cover lost, and his clothing both torn and dirty. But Harry proudly showed a trout that he had brought home for mother's own supper—no one else must ask for a taste or even accept a proffered portion, or cast admiring glances that way. The trout was about five inches long and had a peculiar, ragged appearance. "You see," explained Harry, "the line got tangled after he swallowed the bait, and I shot him for fear he'd get away." "There was no danger of that," said Harry's father. The proud son now expressed a determination to make a fire and cook the trout. "O Harry, don't make a fire to-night and heat the house; the trout will do for breakfast!" "Mother, the housekeeper might eat it herself; little bites; trout is tempting." "No, Harry, she wouldn't do that." "Well, then, mother, I'll dig a hole in the garden and bury the fish to keep it cool all night." "Very well," said she, and Harry spent half an hour in the garden, then came in satisfied with the labors of the day. Throwing himself upon the lounge, he recounted the rambles he had made, how encumbered he had been with so much luggage, the loss of his ramrod, then the theft of his dinner by a hungry dog, and finally how blistered his feet were with so much walking; but he had enjoyed himself. Suddenly he asked, "Do you suppose cats or dogs could burrow under that box?"

He rose, looked out of the window and spied a neighbor's dog sniffing at the fresh earth. That roused him thoroughly and he forgot that he was tired. The dog was chased for a block away; the trout was dug up, the protecting wrappers of paper, cloth, and leaves were removed, a hot fire kindled, and the trout put into the oven. "Baked trout, mother, is a delicacy enjoyed by epicures." "Thank you, Harry, but I'm afraid I can't eat it to-night." "Yes you can, I want you to know what a real fresh brook trout tastes like. I'll practice on my flute while it bakes, and call you when it is done. You go walk in the garden." She had not the heart to refuse his pleading smile, and, glad also to get out of the warm kitchen, she strayed into the front yard, and, oh, what a sight met her gaze! Geraniums, verbenas, and over there the strawberry bed, turned upside down! Holes and mounds of earth, and, lying crossways of a pansy bed, a hoe and long-handled shovel. "What does it mean?" she asked the housekeeper, who was just returning from an errand up town. " He said it was searching for angle-worms, ma'am." Harry's mother re-entered the house after a serious conflict with self, whether to scold or not to scold, and there was he upon the lounge fast asleep after the weariness of the day. She went to the oven; the trout was done like a chip.

When Harry was awakened for bed-time, he said: " Mother, I enjoyed your having that trout more than though I had eaten it myself." " I know it, my son, and now won't you eat some raspberry pie and sweet milk, for I am sure you must be faint?" " Faint! I'm starved! Mother, I couldn't love you more if you were an angel!" Harry concluded this declaration with a rapturous hug, and turned with a boy's own appetite to his tempting meal.

The Oatman Captives.

ABOUT thirty-five years ago, the residents of San Bernardino and Los Angeles Counties were startled by the report that a white woman had been rescued from the Mojave Indians after six years of captivity. This rumor was soon confirmed by the arrival of Miss Olive Oatman, protected by an armed escort of soldiers. She was visited by many persons, and all were interested in her story. It made a deep impression upon my mind, and I will repeat a part of it to you from memory. A company of emigrants set out (from Missouri, I think) for California, but upon the way they became disagreed as to which of two routes was best, so they divided, as Latter-day Saints would not have done. The company in which Mr. Oatman and family traveled also grew discontented, and as they came to small towns one after another stayed behind; but Mr. Oatman was determined to go on alone.

One morning after breakfast, just as they were ready to start, some Apache Indians came to them and demanded food and blankets. Mr. Oatman gave them what he could spare, but they became angry, and in a few moments only Olive and her little sister Mary Ann were to be seen alive. The Indians took what they wished from the wagons, then set them on fire, and, driving the oxen before them, started on foot for the mountains with the girls, Olive, aged twelve, and Mary Ann, eight years old. The younger one soon gave out, her feet becoming so tender from rough walking that at last she was carried upon the back of one Indian, then another, until they arrived in camp, where a great rejoicing was held over the cruel deed. These children were made the drudges of the camp, and were sent out to hunt birds' eggs and grass seeds to eat, also to bring wood and water.

After two years they were sold to the Mojave Indians, among whom their lot was easier, because of kinder treatment. When they had been with this tribe two winters and summers, there came a dry season, and great scarcity prevailed, because the Gila River did not overflow and water their corn and beans. Many Indians died. Little Mary Ann grew weak and then sick, and Olive was permitted to leave work (hunting food) and stay beside her sister. The chief's wife, to whom they had been given, was very kindhearted. She had wisely hidden in the ground some corn for future planting, which the others knew nothing about, and from this store she brought forth a little at a time and gave to the captives privately, not even sharing with her own tribe. As Mary Ann grew nearer death, she talked with Olive, and besought her not to feel utterly alone, but to hope and believe she would yet be released and return to the white people. They had often sung together the hymns they had learned at home, and of these the Indians were very fond, and desired to know the meaning of each line. By and by the certainty of soon parting with her only loved one so overcame Olive that she could not sing, but the little sufferer sang on alone. Oh, think of it, little children in Zion, of that dear child in the desert, who had seen parents, brothers and sisters cruelly slain; who had endured punishment, drudgery, heat, cold and starvation, still remembering the hymns of home, and singing them like a martyr! The last she sang were, "I'm Going Home to Die No More," and "Jesus, Lover of My Soul." The Indians gathered around the death-bed and wept aloud. Mary Ann bade them remember what she and Olive told them of heaven, and bade them good-by. When midnight came, the songs were hushed, the suffering ended.

It was the custom of the Mojaves to burn their dead, but permission was given Olive to bury her sister, and the Indians helped her to dig the grave and heap rocks upon it.

You may feel sure that Olive was now sadder and lonelier than ever.

One day, long after this, as the sun was sinking from sight, a Yuma Indian named Francisco came into camp with a letter from the commanding officer at Fort Yuma, addressed, "To Olivia, a white woman, said to be a prisoner among the Indians." Of course the red men could not understand it, and the letter was handed to Olive to read aloud. It had been so long since she had seen a book or letter that she could not at first read it, and, telling them so, she asked for time to study it out. Within an hour she was able to

do so. It was to the effect that Francisco was author-
ized to purchase her and bring her to the fort.

The Mojaves formed a circle with Francisco and,
Olive standing in the center beside a small fire, and,
thus surrounding her, debated through the long hours
of the night. Some were for killing messenger and
captive, others were anxious for the ransom. Olive
knew that any sign of joy on her part would be to
her injury, and preserved a stoical appearance. Francisco told her in English that a refusal from the tribe
to release her would bring extermination upon them.
He told them that they had only this one night to
deliberate; by morning he must be gone, and they
must decide now.

As daylight came over the hill, they reluctantly
named their price: One horse, seven pairs of blankets,
and five pounds of beads, to be paid on the arrival of
Olive and Francisco at the fort. As the sun appeared,
the circle broke and the two stepped forth free, after
standing through the long night in council. After a
slight breakfast, they set forth, accompanied by the
Indians who were to receive the pay, also the chief's
daughter-in-law, who seemed to love Olive, for she
wept bitterly, as did also some of the children.

At the end of the third day, the sentry at Fort
Yuma discovered their approach, and an escort came
out to meet them. The flag was flying, the band
played, and the cannon boomed. Olive suddenly remembered that she wore only a skirt made of grass,
and sank in confusion to the sand. A gallant soldier

brought a cloak and threw around her, begging her to rise. Olive was received at the gate of the fort by the commanding officer, General Hentzelman, if I remember rightly, and was conducted to the wife of an officer. Soon clothed in female attire, Olive returned to the table awaiting her, where her welcome and her own joy were beyond the feeble powers of language to express.

In a short time after this Olive, attended by a military escort, entered San Bernardino, and next day proceeded to Los Angeles, sixty miles further. There a large crowd awaited her. Her name and story had been passed from lip to lip, and one after another grasped her hand and offered their congratulations upon her escape from that long, sad captivity. One young man hurriedly approached her and asked, "Olive, do you remember your brother Lorenzo?" What a joyous meeting, and how the crowd hurrahed when she answered him with tears of joy! Then he told her that he was left for dead after being thrown over a steep bank, but was awakened to consciousness by the howling of coyotes around him. He crawled up the bank, looked upon the scene of desolation, and then drew himself along the road, back to where he remembered there was water. After drinking and bathing his face, some Pima Indians came that way, found him, and took him home, treating him kindly. After his recovery, he traveled from place to place, believing that all his kindred were slain, until the glad tidings and the arrival of his lost sister. How nobly he would have striven for their release had he only known they were living, and how many brave men would have gone to their rescue!

Olive was tattooed upon her chin, but was a sensible-looking, dignified young woman. Our delegate to the Legislature was the Hon. Jefferson Hunt, a captain in the famous Mormon battalion, and he presented a petition that the State make an appropriation to Olive Oatman, which I think was done.

A minister wrote from Olive's dictation the story of her family's massacre and her own and sister's long captivity, and it was published by her friends.

It was said afterward that Olive married and had a home of comfort and happiness, which Lorenzo shared with her. I have often wished that the grave of little Mary Ann could be found and properly cared for; but God knows where it is, and one day the little martyr will rise rejoicing and meet her own.

The Maricopas and Mojaves told Olive many things that the Latter-day Saints can understand. They knew that their ancestors were once powerful and lived in fine houses, and often pointed to her a certain mountain that none of them would venture near on account of sacred treasures they said were hidden there until a certain future time.

The Haughty Countess and the Slipper.

THE titles of rank sound very fine and seem calcu-
lated to claim our respect. It is supposed that these
honorary distinctions were originally intended to represent a reward for meritorious services or nobility of
character instead of merely distinguishing position
and wealth, as is often now the case. These titled
persons would appear at first thought to be possessed
of superior qualities of mind and heart, compared
with those less favored by birth and education. By
the influences of their elegant surroundings and the
guarded removal from their observations of the inferior phases of human nature, they certainly ought
to develop a higher degree of moral excellence than
those who have struggled through adversity to manhood and womanhood by their own efforts chiefly.
But it appears after all that human nature is very
much the same, either in exalted or lowly positions,
notwithstanding all the lessons and examples with
which life abounds. I will tell you a story in which
this is shown.

Once in Denmark there lived a rich gentleman, a
widower, with an only daughter about ten years of
age. The count possessed large estates by inheritance
from both his parents, and his little daughter also was
heiress to fine property both in city and country, from

her dear, dead mother.   The different suites of house-
servants, laborers, and tenants were all comfortable
and happy with their master, whom they regarded as
the perfect standard of a nobleman.   The little daughter was loved by them all, and they looked forward to
her coming years of womanhood with fond pride.
Little Thyra was happy, for she had as governess and
companion a gentle, Christian lady, her mother's own
cousin, but in humble circumstances, and the two
were much attached to each other.

It had long been said that it was a pity the fine
house should be so quiet, for since the death of the
lovely countess, Olga, six years before, no festivities
had filled the great house, and the few figures that
graced the elegant lawns, gardens, and drives, were
those of the count and his little household.   At last
it was told that their master was about to choose a
bride, and close attention was paid to discover whom
he seemed most to admire.   After a while it was
thought that he paid most attention to a certain elegant lady (also a countess), very handsome and wealthy,
but so imperial in her bearing toward even her equals
that this prospect was met with a lack of that enthusiasm and pleasure that oftenest prevail among the
dependents of a noble family.   Then it was announced
that a fine ball was to be given by the count, at which,
it was hinted, he would make known the lady of his
choice.

Of course great interest prevailed, and many were
the onlookers as the carriages rolled to the ancient

mansion in the ancient park beside the lake. The
grounds as well as the house were illuminated, also
the boats upon the water, from which bands discoursed
sweet music echoing back to that in the dancing-hall.
Little Thyra stood beside her father until all the guests
had been welcomed, then wandered to the side of the
governess, who had been invited to be present in attendance upon her. A little while before supper was
announced, the beautiful countess, who prided herself
that she had already received marked attention over
all other ladies, from the master of the house, began
to display unusual vivacity of spirit. All at once she
noticed that the silken string of her embroidered satin
slipper was loose, and, seizing this opportunity to display her power, called to the little Thyra, as she stood
with one foot imperiously forward: "Come her, child,
and tie my shoe-string." Thyra looked up into the
proud beauty's face calmly, but made no movement.
The countess regarded her with heightened color and
flashing eyes that boded ill for the future happiness of
the child. "Come here, you silly little goose, and tie
the string of my slipper." While many gazed in quiet
surprise, and Thyra looked suffused with shame, thus
addressed, the governess left her seat, and, advancing,
knelt before her: "I will tie your slipper-string, my
lady." The baffled countess replied so low that few
heard her: "You will not be here long; you have
trained that child, but I will humble her."

Thyra paled at the thought of a separation from her
kind governess, but said nothing. The count was a

silent witness and faintly smiled, none being able to discover his thought.   When, a few moments later, he spoke to Thyra, her eyes drooped and filled with tears, but she overcame the emotion and was calm as before.

Strangely, it seemed to all, the count took his little daughter to the table and seated her at his left hand with her governess next below her. " Ah!" whispered the guests, "he will make known his choice when the dancing begins."   The supper passed merrily to its end, when the count spoke: "My friends, I have promised to make known to-night the lady whom I have chosen to grace my house, bless my life, and be a mother to my child."   With these words he arose, and, extending his hand to the governess, asked, "Will you accept the trust?"   Little Thyra caught the trembling white hand, and, with pleading, brimming eyes, placed it in her father's, who lifted it to his lips, then, drawing it through his arm, passed from the room with the gentle lady and Thyra to the grand dancing-hall.   When all were seated, it was observed that the haughty countess had vanished.

It needs hardly to be told that, through all the count's broad estates, there was rejoicing at the wisdom of his choice.   The Countess Caroline adorned her new position with the same gentle grace that had won the respect and affection of the household when herself in a dependent position, and the ardent love of the gentle child, to whom she had been teacher, friend, and guide.

The choice bridal gift of pearls from her husband

was truly appropriate to the purity of her spirit; and the radiant faces of her husband's tenantry showed how fervent was their welcome. As they left the church, the gentle shower that had come, passed away, and before them, over the park and the ancient mansion, a rainbow rested like a triumphal arch through which they should pass, and like a benison of heaven. The happy people round about at sight of the sign lifted their voices in unison in expressions of delight at the happy and beautiful omen, so full of promise and of peace; but what the haughty countess thought at her window far away, none ever heard or cared to know.

"He Maketh the Rain to Fall in Small Drops."

THE title of this subject is from the Bible. When I first read this line, I did not at the moment see anything very special in it; but if we study the Scriptures closely, we find that there is no line amiss, nor any waste words. I may add that I believe any reasonable question may be answered out of the Bible. When you know a close reader of that sacred Book, you know one who is always prepared with a conclusive answer to any important question, and such a reader is always known as a wise person.

I think that the full meaning of the words that I have quoted were not so apparent to me before as after the great and awful flood at Johnstown, Pennsylvania. Many other equally disastrous inundations occurred in other parts of the earth at nearly the same time, but the one named will suffice to prove the meaning I have in view. The waters did not "fall in small drops" upon that place; if they had done so, what a blessing instead of a disaster! Imagine the result, if every time it rained the water should come down in bucketfuls! Fruit would be destroyed, branches broken, leaves stripped off, grass and all small plants would be washed out by the roots, paths ruined by holes washed out in them. Dear me! where would trouble end or anything be left? Imagine being out in such a shower, and such large *drops* coming down upon you!

Can you not see the mercy and tenderness of causing "the rain to fall in small drops"? Could we throw a pail of water up in the air, or stand on a height and pour it down so that it would "fall in small drops"? This is one example where the power of God differs from ours. He has many ways of managing water where we have but few. He can cause it to fall in such a delicate manner that the tiniest flowers are refreshed but not crushed, and their gently and instantly distilled delicate odors ascend between the falling drops and perfume the atmosphere. Often, after a shower, you will find flowers and even leaves, each holding a single sparkling drop of rain like a jewel flashing in the sun.

Many a spear of grass bending and quivering in the gently-moving breeze, balances upon its tip a shining drop.

Such sights as these have been imitated by the most skillful flower-makers for the wreaths and sprays that adorn feminine head-wear; and even queens have sought to have these beauties of nature reproduced in their richest jewels. Is it not wonderful and beautiful? And instead of children spending time studying unprofitable things, if they would employ the same time and diligence in perusing the Scriptures, asking God to open their minds that they might understand, how much better it would be! The Lord says he loves those who speak of him and seek after his knowledge.

"In small drops." And yet by these fields are moistened, trees nourished and grow into giants, fish and many great creatures are sheltered and fed, rivers, lakes, and seas are formed. God has even fought great battles (as when the hosts of the Egyptians were overthrown and drowned in the Red Sea), and he has punished whole cities for disobeying his laws by covering them with these "small drops," and once—the whole earth! We may well pause and wonder at the mighty meaning conveyed in those few words, "He maketh the rain to fall in small drops." And if so much is contained in one line, how much more, if comprehended, does the whole Bible contain!

Once I used to be greatly distressed by the high winds that prevail at some periods of the year. This fear increased, so that whenever a strong wind arose,

17

the hours of night were one long suspense to me. Often I would walk around the room, feeling the walls to ascertain how much the house was shaking. One night I could bear my own thoughts no longer, and lighted the lamp, then opened the Bible.

The first line I read was like this : "I will lie down in peace; for thou, O Lord, makest me to sleep in safety." These words had such power and conviction to my heart that I immediately returned to my bed, and sank into a peaceful slumber. Never since that time have such fears distressed me. No assurances of friends, no inspector of buildings, and no strong walls, could have done me the good that I received from that one line of Scripture.

" Thou Shalt Not Be Afraid."

MORE than twenty years ago while crossing the deserts from California to Utah, I had another proof that in the Bible may all things be found. There was a train of perhaps forty wagons. It was my custom to carry a pocket Bible, which I consulted during the day as we traveled. One morning I opened upon this verse: "Thou shalt not be afraid for the terror by night, nor for the arrow that flieth by day." How does that apply? We are at peace with the Indians, I thought; but before midnight we were attacked, and all our animals were away in a herd in the hills, in care of the Indians. There was much alarm in camp, for four Indians had been shot, and there was a narrow canyon to go through next day, and forty miles to the next watering-place. We were kept awake the rest of the night, for now and then a bullet from the enemy would strike our wagons. But the promise in those lines was fulfilled, although we were closely followed all the next day, and when we reached the Muddy River, a long line of red men stood between us and the water. However, they let us pass through. Those sacred words were like a warning and promise hours before the danger came.

The Esquimaux.

WHEN winter comes, we think it necessary to have a good, tight, warm house to keep out the cold and make us comfortable.

The dwelling of the Esquimaux is built of blocks of clear ice cemented together by pouring melted snow between them, and a thinner one is inserted for a window to let in light, not to see through. The beds are made of moss and the soft fur skins of the polar bear. Long ropes of sinews stretched overhead form a place to put their clothing and weapons for hunting and fishing. Their only fire is a stone lamp with whale-

THE ESQUIMAUX.

oil and twisted moss for a wick. This does not afford
enough heat to melt the ice walls. Over the lamp
they slightly cook their bear and walrus meat. Sometimes food is so scarce that, when a hunt has been
successful, they will tear off strips of flesh and devour
it raw.

An Esquimaux baby or child never knows the taste
of candy or sweets as you do; a clean piece of fat is
their especial treat. They never see a doll, ribbon,
laces, toys or picture-books; their only trinkets of
adornment are a few beads purchased from voyagers,
and these they prize as you would a costly necklace.
They never heard of a concert, theater, or May-day
picnic; never saw beautiful flowers on tree or grass,
and very seldom go visiting, so have few acquaintances. These children know nothing of cake, pie, fruit
or nuts, or change of fashions. I don't suppose they
have soap, either.

The mothers carry their babes in something such
cradles as Indians use, only the child is wrapped in
many furs. An Esquimaux baby has to be very good,
for its mother has to sew skins instead of cloth, with
a large bone, home-made needle, and sinews for thread,
and it must be slow and heavy work, but she does it
so neatly that the clothing is water-tight. She also
mends the fishing lines, boats, and leather covering of
the little pointed boats that sometimes get torn on the
floating ice. Only one person can sit in a boat, and
he squeezes into that through a place left in the center, sitting so securely that boat and man seem as one.

They travel over the ice in sleds drawn by dogs, and go very swiftly. They are not as kind to these useful and faithful creatures as they should be. Many children are ungrateful and unsatisfied with what indulgent parents have provided for them, but they would be sorry to change places with the little Esquimaux. How thankful we should be for the changing seasons of spring, summer, fall and winter, for all the beauties and bounties they afford, and for the comforts and advantages of civilized life! Whether we possess them or not, much is learned by *seeing* the productions of wealth, labor, and art. Everyone who makes a beautiful thing or teaches an idea, benefits the multitude as well as himself. We should be thankful for the houses of worship and education, and the knowledge that floods the earth through the power of the printing-press, all of which is unknown to the little Esquimaux. The poorest child has reason to be thankful that he was not born to dwell in the almost perpetual desolations of snow and ice. Yet they have a sort of enjoyment in their way, and do not murmur that their lot is so hard. Perhaps, sometime, God will bring them forth to a better state of existence upon this earth, for they too are his children. I would like to see one of these poor creatures brought from that solitude and taken from one place to another, from the great busy wharves into the wonderful manufactories of cities, the beautiful parks, and the fresh country farms. How I would love to witness their surprise and delight!

When you have a "Merry Christmas" or other happy time, think of the little Esquimaux, and thank God that you were born in a pleasant part of the world, and brought to a knowledge of His greatness, His manifold works, power and love.

"Ma Likes Me."

THERE was once a little boy of four years who was very unfortunate in having a disposition to do just the wrong thing instead of the right one. He required constant watching, being so forgetful of all the admonitions he had received; it seemed almost of no use to talk to him. If the chickens were securely locked into their own inclosure, they were generally to be found soon after, scratching in the garden. If the milk-closet was properly closed, somebody had the mysterious faculty of letting a swarm of flies in, which cook might discover at her leisure. No matter if cook gave him a handful of cakes and a glass of milk while dinner was getting ready, this little fellow could not refrain from slyly nipping the cake or pie, and tasting the honey or preserves, as signs upon the tablecloth proved. It was "somebody" who added extra bluing to the rinse water when the washerwoman's back was turned, and who was it had pulled the melons before they were ripe? and who—well, there was no end of perplexing questions that never were quite answered, and all the time a certain little boy was looking the picture of innocence. But at last questionings ceased and accusations were the order, and after a while this small boy used to receive lectures,

"MA LIKES ME."

and be asked often enough "where he thought he was going to by and by if he did not change his course." This oft-repeated question seemed to have no rousing effect upon him, for he always made the same reply, that he "didn't know;" and I don't suppose that his questioners could have answered any better if it had been left to them. Well, after spools of colored thread had been unraveled and tangled ruinously, the machine-oil can hopelessly spiked with needles, and auntie's lovely lace pattern unraveled "to see the crinkles in the thread," the assembled ladies—mother, auntie, and a guest, with such onlookers as cook and laundress—began to talk to him again, more impressively than ever, if possible.

Auntie said the most, and her remarks received expressiveness and indorsement from the uplifted hands of the laundress, the frowns, shakes of the head, and the declaration of the cook that "that child almost outdid hisself in contrariness." "Who can love you?" "Love him! who can even like him?" "See what you've done. Who would have such a boy? Not I, as a gift." "Nor I, if I was paid for it." Things began to look dark for somebody, as he looked from one face to another. In mother's look he discovered not indignation, but sorrow, and felt a little of the heavy feeling removed. "Why don't you say something, bad boy?" said auntie, and, thus urged, he braved up and answered, "Ma likes me." How could ma deny this and destroy his only dependence?

That thought was something he could lean back upon, though all around were against him. Ma beckoned him to her, took him out, washed the ink-marks from his fingers, put a clean apron on him, and

just asked him, "Now won't you try to be good?"
He promised, and all the afternoon was the most uneasy being imaginable, trying to keep his word; and
it tired him so that he fell asleep before three o'clock.

Pictures in the Sand.

OH, in he came a-dancing,
  As happy as could be,
But what was all the matter
  I could not hear or see.

"Can't you keep still a moment,
  So I can understand?"
"We've been having our pictures taken!"
  "Where?"   "Yonder in the sand."

"In a row, all holding hands,
  We laid still as could be,
And Tom marked all around us
  And ended off with me."

"I'd like to see the pictures."
  He answered with a shout
Of happy fun and laughter,—
  "We've gone and rubbed 'em out."

Delicacy of Feeling.

THE value of a charitable deed depends entirely
upon the way it is done. Remember, the poor are
always sensitive. Said a poor woman: "If anyone
gives me anything and then tells of it, *I've paid for
it.*" Yes, paid for it in shame and distress more than
the gift was worth. Said a lady at her gate one day:

"That's Mrs. Dean; I know it's her by her dress. I gave it to her."

Once one man said to another, "I gave you this work because you were poor and I thought you'd be glad to get it." Why did he remind the man of his distress, already hard to bear? It would have sounded much better if he had said: "It is very handy getting this work done so near home. I am glad you could do it for me." The workman would have thought: "I like to work for him, his manners are so pleasant."

Now judge which is nicest. A lady was having the Primary Association girls at her house to make a quilt for a donation to some worthy object. One girl whispered: "My sister and I are the only ones here without white aprons." She did not know it was overheard till after dinner, when the hostess appeared from an inner room and whispered to her, "Now you're not the only ones with gingham aprons on." I heard the whisper, glanced at the two faces, and lovelier smiles I never saw. They were from the hearts of sympathy and appreciation.

The Lost Art of Patchwork.

I HAVE been led to think (from my observations among my young acquaintances) that one of the pretty domestic arts is going out altogether. There is such a spirit of buying things ready-made, to save work and time. I never see a home-woven bed-

spread or pretty patchwork quilt but that I have a
kindly feeling for the maker. I know some·gentlemen,
sensible ones, who feel the same way.

I remember how sweet and attractive looked a
bevy of tidy, happy girls; they had done up all the
forenoon's work, and left a quiet, cool house for
mother, and were spending their spare afternoon in
industriously putting together fanciful blocks, comparing, and learning patterns from each other, someone now and then enlivening the rest by a sweet or
merry song, and all enjoying themselves the while
they accomplished something useful.

Once I saw a lady buying calico in short lengths,
and she explained to the clerk that they were for
patchwork. "Who is going to make patchwork?"
he inquired. "My daughters." "Is it possible! I
did not know of any girls that did that kind of
work nowadays. I thought that was one of the lost
arts. I'd like to get acquainted with girls of that
kind."

I remember a very rich gentleman who paid a high
price for a quilt of the "Irish chain" pattern. When
I expressed my surprise, he said: "Not all the silk
and velvet curtains or the upholstered furniture in my
residence can call up such beautiful thoughts for me
as when I enter my room I see that red and white
quilt, and my rest is all the sweeter when I know this
is over me. I see and hear many things that were
once long ago in my own country, and I will keep
this so long as I live."

Another gentleman, sick for many months, one day asked if he could have a patchwork quilt on his bed, he was so tired of a white one. So when it was brought, he smiled and wanted us to "tell him all the pieces." Said he, "My mother once made a patchwork quilt just for me, and I knew all the pieces by heart." I am quite sure that the study of that quilt did much to take his mind from his sickness, and when he was well again he regretted parting with it, so the quilt became his property.

Now, girls, take any patchwork quilt you have, the older it is the better, and look back to the time you made it, and who was at the quilting. Who made the pies and cake? Who got the "wish-bones"? Did you gather up the quilt and throw it over somebody's head, saying, "It's your turn next," creating confusion and fun? Did you clear everything away after supper and have a little dancing? Do you remember who of the beaux came to take the girls home? Are the pretty fingers that quilted it still warm and quick in life? or are some of those friendly hands whiter than ever before, and still?

Pleasure and industry, usefulness and comfort, the past and the present, all are stitched in and folded up into that precious patchwork quilt.

Prince Tape, His Reign and Death.

ONCE, long ago and far away, in a country whose name was never seen upon any map, there lived a prince who ruled with absolute sway over his subjects, none of whom presumed to question his authority, or ventured to intercede for mercy in judgment. Absolute individual power is not the wisest form of government for ordinary mortals, but its being Prince Tape's right by birth he felt that it was perfectly lawful for him to exercise it. So, by degrees, he became more and more tyrannical, and when he had brought all his human and animal subjects under perfect control, he brought his magical power to bear upon the birds of the air, the fishes of the sea, and even the trees, grasses, winds and waters. You see, he could not be satisfied. All these were commanded to acknowledge his presence by profound obeisance; the birds to dart swiftly before him, the trees and grasses to bow low, the fishes to form in double line through which his vessel was rowed, and the winds to sigh or loudly roar, as his mood or temper demanded. It would seem that Prince Tape had everything so that he was master over all things. But there is always a power behind a power, although we cannot see it, and there never was a good man but that there was a better one, so there never was a tyrant but that there was a greater one. All things have their allotted time and sphere, especially bad ones. Our humblest servant

might, on opportunity, become our sternest master.
None of these ideas seemed to have entered Prince
Tape's mind, and perhaps if they had he would have
scorned them.   But Prince Tape's despotic plans were
not his own; they entered his mind from somewhere,
just as the air we breathe is not of our own creating
but comes from a boundless source.   So the despotism
of Prince Tape came by the prompting of Prince Evil,
who was trying to see how many stern things he
could urge him to perform.   By and by Prince Evil,
who was invisible to the eyes of mortals, felt an intense desire to persecute Prince Tape, as that tyrant
had treated others, and when Prince Evil has a design,
he is strong enough to carry it out if, as in Prince
Tape's case, he had no claim for assistance or mercy.
So Prince Evil began a warfare from his higher seat
of power, and soon Prince Tape was put to flight from
his strong castle, and sought to hide himself, but, so
accustomed had been his subjects to do him reverence,
with no thought that he could be dethroned, that in
his efforts to escape they pointed the way of his flight
instead of concealing it.

His human subjects prostrated themselves before
him; the animals, tame and wild, turned their heads to
look which way he had gone; birds darted before him;
trees and grasses bowed low as before, and when at
length he leaped into the deep waters to escape his
great enemy, the beautiful fishes circled around him,
the waves leaped and foamed, and the winds roared.
Then the spirit of evil, whose home was in the black

clouds above him, threw lances of lightning that pierced him to the death. Thus you see the tyranny he had exercised became his own executioner.

This is only an allegory, to show us how, if we could have our own way in all things, and are selfish and cruel to others, we may triumph in our own power for a while, but a higher power will in turn delight in our destruction, and we have formed the weapons to assist him. Do unto others as we would have them do unto us, and we will have friends not foes in time of need.

The Dead Grape-vine.

You say, "Dig up this old vine and burn it; it is worthless." Did you but know the story of this gray stump and brittle branches, you would recall the last words, for what has once been of use and beauty can never be worthless. We do not speak so of dead great men, and a vine is an object of worth in its own sphere. Let me tell you the story of this old grape-vine, and learn whether it does not deserve your gentle respect.

To begin with, it has been quite a traveler, and came of a high family, in a lovely country you have never seen. Far away on the fairy-like coast of a tropical land, there flourished a vineyard more than a hundred years old, a vineyard that had outlived three kings, and had quietly pursued its appointed destiny, while countries waged war against each other, deluged fields with blood of horses and men, destroyed the grand works of years, and brought sorrow into hearts and homes by the thousand.

But from this vineyard, which escaped destruction, the choicest clusters were plucked for the tables of royalty. Often the peasants filling the baskets have tasted the lesser clusters (such fruit as you and I never tasted under this cold sky); and, oh, how sweet the air was there, how beautiful the scene from the terraces where these vines grew, and what melody rang through the long green rows by day, and the changeful voice of the nightingale when all others were silent! Ah, the native associations of this dead grape-vine were beautiful indeed!

Then someone from our own free America brought away cuttings from those noble vines, and whether all survived in this cold climate I cannot say, but this one, faithful to its ancient name, bore clusters of such fruit as few mortals taste.

He trained it around the porch of the home to which he brought his bride. Here they often sat in the moonlight, and, later, how often they lifted up the baby to catch at the tempting fruit!

How many a cluster has this vine yielded, carrying delight and refreshment to the fevered lips of the sick! How rich have been the dried and pressed bunches in the long winter evenings! and tiny glasses have sparkled with the rich coloring of their autumn yield.

18

Shade, food, and drink through many a year, a
noble ancestry, beauty and usefulness all its life, these
are what it has given you.

A dead grape-vine! Who will write its epitaph, this
vanished delight?

"I Don't Look Like I Was a Bad Boy."

"Go into the parlor, naughty boy.
  Sit there, and think of what you've done."
What was it? Nothing very bad,
  Only his mischief and his fun;
A spool unraveled, just to see
  How long it would keep coming off;
A pepper-box all sifted out,
  That made the kitty sneeze and cough;

The baby's doll in a slipper fine
  With grandma's letter for a sail,
Tied to a slender stick for mast,
  His boat afloat in the water pail;
Not tall enough to watch his play,
  He stood upon my newest book—
'Twas this I found, when his clear laugh
  Caused me to stop my work and look.

    .   .   .   .   .   .

The parlor door stood just ajar;
  The silence grew too much for me;

"I DON'T LOOK LIKE I WAS A BAD BOY."

I turned about to catch a glimpse
    Of what his penitence might be;
And, seated in his tiny chair,
    Gone from his pretty face its joy,
He murmured to the mirror's truth,
    "I don't look like I was a bad boy."

O precious boy! to think those words
    Could cause thy tender heart to grieve;
Not even angels, when they heard
    The hasty utterance, could believe.
Forever be thy faults as small,
    And but the fruit of thoughtless joy;
Let me kiss back thy smiles again,
    Mother's own precious, dear, good boy!

The Cucumber's Soliloquy.

"I was not born in this place. I well remember
the spot where I first saw the light; there was a warm,
loamy bed; the temperature was summer-like, without
varying night or day, and a sky of glass arched over
me, through which I could see the sun by day, the
moon and stars by night.

"My situation was rendered agreeable by numberless
associates of my own class, and many superiors, whose
more refined and elegant appearance added to our
spirits and growth and revived us from any tendency
to drooping. I was rapidly growing slender and of

a delicate appearance. No rough winds tossed and toughened our leaves. I might have attained to great possibilities, possibly taken a prize at a county fair, if these conditions had continued, but I suppose this idea never entered my master's mind, and I had not the privilege of suggesting it. One day my master, the florist and gardener, entered with an assistant, an inferior person, and said, 'Thomas, it's time to transplant these cucumbers, cabbages, and tomatoes into open ground.' The inferior person replied, 'Please, sir, I think it is.'

"Directions were given where to place us, and we were lifted out with trowels, placed in shallow basket and carried out. Oh, how large the world seemed t us outside the green-house! I soon noticed many new things, fences, trees, birds, and so much outdoors that there seemed no end of view. We were soon set out separately at distances that made us feel lonely, and by nightfall we were shivering in the strange, uncovered garden. I heard Thomas say, 'A good rain, now, would be a benefit.' Well, by morning I had recovered from my drooping, and tried to discover some floral associates, but did not see any. I missed their perfume. The dew had slightly chilled my sensitive frame and I was thankful for the sunrise, but it soon became too hot, and I felt like fainting.

"Before night an alarm aroused us to a new peril. A noisy, fussy creature such as I had never seen before, with a troop of smaller, less dangerous-looking ones, stood over me making a great noise, and then proceeded to tear up the ground in all directions, seeming to find something desirable there. Dirt flew all over me, and some sharp scratches almost lacerated my tender branches beyond recovery, and I don't know but that extermination awaited me, but just at that critical moment the gardener called to Thomas to 'drive that old hen and chickens out of that vegetable patch and shut them up.' Thus were my friends and I spared.

"We rallied from the shocks we had received, and our healthy natures asserted themselves by rapid growth. We had good care from the gardener; he would loosen up the soil so we could stretch out our cramped legs and feet under-ground, and feel the warm sun strike through. Then we would spread our arms over the soft soil and display our green skirts and floral decorations to whomsoever might pass. By and by I heard a pleasant exclamation: 'These vines are just loaded with cucumbers. Now we can count on pickles and salads at home and to sell.' I had thought that these young cucumbers belonged to me, but now fresh troubles began in my mind, for I heard the gardener explain to a green grocer who wanted to contract for hundreds of us, how to make salads, whole pickles and piccalilli, chow-chow and mangoes, till my form swelled with fright and indignation, and I tried to hide under my green mantle. The poor tomatoes, peppers, and purple cabbages were included in the dreadful description of peelings, scaldings, spicings, and choppings. I learned

a great deal in that afternoon, but saw no hope of
escape. The peppers might resent with their fiery
juice, cabbage was pronounced productive of colic,
and sliced green cucumbers were warned against as
being dangerous. Oh, thought I, how much I would
prefer being eaten green! I would then pass away
knowing that retribution would descend upon the
greedy one. But to be peeled alive, sliced and pierced
with spices, and scalded with vinegar, I could not
bear to contemplate it. The slow, lingering process
of being salted down in kegs, only to be taken out,
scalded and drowned in vinegar, then at last to be
sliced and eaten by company, was no better. How I
long to turn tough and yellow before they find me!
I am only half grown. Every day somebody stands
over me impatiently waiting for me to grow faster. I
hear them blame cats for killing birds to eat, but they
think it all right to eat me. Hark! it is the gardener
and Thomas, each with a bushel basket, wheelbarrow,
and sharp scissors. I feel that my time of life here
is drawing to a close, and I know not whither I shall
be hurried."

Just at this moment I saw the two men approaching, and the listener to this soliloquy hastily left the
premises, having no satisfactory explanation to make
for his presence between the cucumber and melon
patches.

The Magician.

THIS is a fairy story, but it is a true one, as you will know when I have done.

Magicians are not believed in nowadays, but they still exist, and I will tell you about one whom you can all employ after reading my story.

A favored being of earth, endowed with the spirit and power of which I speak, once exclaimed, "I wish!" And he wished to see a city built, to see forests and fields, streams, tiny lakes, and many other wonderful things, in a desolate country. This power was put into force in a thousand directions, and soon dwellings arose, scenes once barren waste became endless beauty, human creatures and dumb animals rejoiced, and the abundance of all good things brought harmony in every home, and there was no envy, for this power blessed all alike. I saw this power in its might and beauty, and it was not from beneath, it was from above; it was a principle that even exalted beings recognize, honor, and employ. Idleness, want, and misery had vanished, and the thoughts of human creatures had time to soar to loftier themes that still had in them the higher demands of this motive power. Shall I tell you the secret, that you also may exercise this magical gift? The lowliest hearts and hands may wield it and help to adorn the earth, help to ennoble and bless each fellow-creature. The name of this magical power is Prayerful Labor.

The Enchanted City.

THE sunset's hue had faded out,
And soft gray shadows fell about;
All faintly traced the outlines stood,
And, velvet-like, the cool green wood.

His feet were tired, and drearily
He thought of night. All cheerily
A little brook spoke up to him
From 'neath a tree's cool shade and dim,
And by the well-worn path he knew
Some dwelling must be near it too.

The shadows softer, quicker fell,
Then one by one, as by a spell.
The glimmering lights waked here and there
Like stars below; home lights so fair
To those who own such haven blest,
Where waiteth welcome, joy, and rest.

Then, as the traveler nearer drew,
A sweet sound charmed his spirit through,
An evening hymn of gratitude
That cheered his weary solitude.

"I will not venture to their door;
'Tis but a little distance more
Where shines another cheerful light;
There will I seek for rest to-night."
But as he neared the second place
A hymn rose to the throne of grace.

The wanderer paused, then far and near,
Like wind-harps, changeful, sweet, and clear,
Faint strains of music rose and fell
And wrought around his soul a spell.
"Am I a-dream, or lost, or where,
That all the nightfall seems to bear
Music afloat on every hand,
Or have I found a fairy-land?"

Then one belated, answered him:
"It is the hour for evening hymn
Through all the land, the call to prayer.
Come, pilgrim, haste, I must be there,
For now each soul with one accord
Returns its praise unto the Lord."

'Twas but a dream! Oh, were it so,
Our peace would like a river flow!
Happy that time if there might be
Such law of grace and harmony
That at the lamp-light's given hour
Each heart would render to this power
Acknowledgments of blessings won
Throughout the day just past and gone.

Then would His blessing and His care
Make each night calm and each day fair;
Then would their truth to God be known,
And He delight to bless His own.

The Gold Miner.

THIS picture shows you a part of one of the processes by which gold is taken from the earth. This miner is working a "placer" mine, which means that

the gold found is in grains or nuggets either on or near the surface of the ground. The miner shovels earth into a broad, flat pan, then holds it partly under water, shaking the pan gently so that the dirt washes away, while the gold, being heavier, sinks to the bottom. Then he pours out the gold and begins with another pan of dirt. Sometimes a pan will yield only a few cents of pure gold, but even then it pays the miner. He sits patiently all day, week in and out, month after month. Often he has a partner, and they take turns in digging and carrying the earth to the water. Sometimes it is carried in strong sacks on a mule's or donkey's back down a mountain-side.

THE GOLD MINER.

Sometimes they find large nuggets worth dollars or even hundreds of dollars apiece. Often the nuggets are so beautiful in shape that a jeweler need only to attach a pin, and there is a beautiful and valuable scarf-pin.

If you should see a gold miner traveling, you would not think he looked like a rich man—his blankets, flour, bacon, pick-ax, shovel, gold-pan, coffee-pot, and frying-pan, all strapped onto the back of a horse, which he leads, while he rides another, if he can afford two animals. Often the miner is robbed of his hard earnings and has to go back and patiently work again.

Many a man, tempted by reports of rich mines, has left home hoping to become suddenly rich. They have endured the burning heat and the furious storms of outdoor life, dangers from wild animals, desperate men and sickness, all for the love of gold. Very few have endured so much for religion.

Miners who have met disappointment wander from place to place, always in need but ever hopeful. These are called "prospectors," and many of them have never found the mines of which they talked and dreamed. Many a one has never gone back to the home he left, but has died far away "in camp." They have washed away mountain-sides, turned streams out of their beds, and in the crevices of the rocks found rich streaks of gold. The eye of a prospector is ever looking downward for signs of gold, the color of earth and rock, or for "float." But you do not know what float is. Well, when a prospector finds a pebble that

has a sign of gold in it, he looks around for more. If
it was on a hill-side, he says, "That rolled down," and
he starts up the hill, carefully watching for more of
the same kind. He may find the ledge of rock it was
loosened from, then, hurrah! Now his anxieties are
over, now he is going to be a millionaire, now he is
going to make them all rich at home and he is going
to put on style. But stop; he must stake off his
claim, put up a notice, and work, no telling how long.
Perhaps someone will "jump his claim" and drive him
away or rob and kill him. So the poor miner may
never realize riches after all, never gladden the hearts
at home.

Placer mining is the simplest and cheapest. Quartz
mining is where the gold is in clear white rock, sometimes in beautiful veins or branches, so beautiful that
jewelry is made from the cut and polished stone.
Heavy machinery is used to crush and grind this
quartz rock, and the fine gold is then by skillful process taken from it.

Once a lady and her husband ran a race in the gold
business. He went to the mines, worked in all kinds
of weather, had the rheumatism, was poisoned by
poison-oak, bitten by snakes and chased by bears, then
was robbed of all the gold he had not sent home by
express.

His wife started a chicken ranch and sold eggs for
six dollars a dozen, sold milk and butter, melons, also,
at five dollars apiece. Then she made dried-apple pies
for one dollar each, and cookies one dollar a dozen.

Oh, how good her cooking tasted to the poor fellows who had been living on bacon and flapjacks! When the year was up, the lady had the most money, and hadn't gone from home to earn it. Their property was improved, and everything looked so good to the tired husband that he said, "My home is the best 'claim' in the mountains."

When the "gold fever" settles upon a man, it is one of the very worst to cure. Years ago when emigrants by the thousand passed through Utah to California, many of the poor pioneers here felt a desire to go also. Pres. Brigham Young advised them to stay here and make good homes. A few who went became rich and returned to their families, but more of them were too poor to get back without help from their friends here, and some died there. Not every man who goes to the mines is sure of making a fortune, and it was proved in many cases that where gold was so easily gained it went fast.

There is a worldliness of spirit, an excitement, and so many influences different from ordinary life, in gold mining, that the heart is slowly and insensibly led away from studious reflections, from Sabbath observances and self-searching of the heart. Among strangers, adrift as it were, and each one for himself, a few months can change a good citizen into another person. Perhaps he will say, "I'm no worse than the rest;" but he may have changed the true gold of a once pure life for the gold of earth, which thieves may steal away—and then what is left? Only a gold miner, shabby and poor indeed.

Envy Defeated.

MANY years ago, in Denmark, there was a workman in the ship-building yards belonging to the government. In that country, dishonesty is severely punished. This man was a workman of more than ordinary ability, and after a while his comrades began to envy him, for he was never out of work, and, being temperate and frugal, he was becoming better off than some others who spent their earnings freely.

The carpenter had a wife and one daughter about twenty years of age, and they lived in a humble cottage, very neat and as attractive as their means and labor could make it, from gateway to fireside.

After a few weeks of discontent, the workmen concocted a plan for the overthrow of this carpenter. A few large nails were slipped into his jacket pocket after he had laid it aside, and then the charge of theft was preferred against him, to the superintendent. A search was ordered, and the nails were found. It was inferred that this petty thieving might have been going on a long time, and as the testimony of his comrades was all unfavorable to him, he was sentenced to a term of imprisonment. This also meant loss of work in the future, for, his good name being gone, who would employ him?

When the news came to the little cottage, the surprise and distress of the mother and daughter were beyond words to describe, but they would not believe the accusation. After some time spent in weeping and wondering, the daughter became calm, and assured her mother that she was going to make an effort to obtain her father's honorable release. She took a small sum of money and went to a shop. On her return she entreated her mother to retire to bed and be prepared to aid her on the morrow. Fervent prayer was offered up, and the mother went to her own room. All night a light burned, and in the morning the dutiful daughter awakened her parent to rise and partake of coffee and bread. After their frugal meal, the mother went to the door and looked down the long lane where for so many years her husband had come and gone to his work. Sad thoughts and fears were filling her mind, when her daughter stood before her, clad in simple white, her beautiful hair loosened and covering her shoulders like a silken cloak. "The king comes through the forest to-day; I will speak to him." The mother clasped the girl to her heart and with a caress and blessing released her. It was so early that the street was still and the girl hastened on to the forest, no one observing her at that hour.

The good king, with his brave attendants, was riding merrily along when, suddenly, from behind a thicket, stepped forward a girl in white, and knelt before them.

Some cried "Danger!" and would have hurried her from the presence of the king, but he ordered that the girl be heard before judging so hastily.

Accordingly, the story of her father's trouble was

related, and the king's face wore an expression that none could understand. "What is your name?" "Hilma, your Majesty." "Will you conduct me to your home?" the king asked, and Hilma joyfully answered, "Yes," and led the way. Then the king alighted, and, throwing his bridle over his arm, walked beside the village girl through the forest to her humble door. His attendants, following the example of their king, followed in quiet procession, a strange and new sight to the villagers.

Entering, he greeted the mother with kindness, assuring her that he would personally inquire into the matter, then rode away.

Very soon, the officers of the law before whom the case was tried, the witnesses and prisoner were brought before the king. Then the king, in a low voice that none heard, said a few words to the carpenter that shook him with surprise; and while all wondered, the king proclaimed him a free man, and they went out side by side back to the little cottage.

Can you imagine the joy of those who watched them approaching? Once again within the walls of that lowly home, and while his courtiers waited without, the king asked the girl a question which sent the color to her face, then left her pale and trembling. She looked at her father, and met a steadfast, approving look in his face. "Accept it, my daughter, in gratitude and joy, for what has not our king done for his poor servants!" "Nay, my friend, not as a debt of gratitude, for justice was your right; but if this maiden

19

can give me her heart, I will give her all I can bestow
but a place beside me on my throne, and my subjects
will understand and honor her in her position, and for
her deed as a daughter."

Hilma understood the nature of a morganatic mar-
riage. Then, as she looked in the face of the king,
she thought how handsome and noble, how gentle and
good of heart he was, to listen to her petition—who
would not love him?—and knew that she could have
loved him if he had never been a king, and she extended to him her hand. The king took from his own
hand a jeweled ring, and placed it on her finger, then
he rode away with all his grand men.

Very soon after this, Hilma was married to the king
" with the left hand," which means a wife of second degree. The king provided fine estates and a title for
Hilma, and made legal provisions for their children, if
God should so bless them. The parents were removed far from their old associates to a home near
their daughter; and those who lately hated them, and
would have caused their ruin, would have been very
humble and respectful if they could have approached
them.

The good queen had never been blessed with an
heir to the throne, and the king and she had often
mourned that they had no dear little one to caress, for
such feelings are natural to every true heart; also they
knew that their name would die out, and another family would succeed to the throne when they were gone.
So this noble queen had given her consent that if he

could find some pure-hearted, proven maiden, he should take her.

When the king told her of Hilma, she expressed a desire to look upon her, unknown to the humble girl. Accordingly, one day Hilma was taken to a picture-gallery, and while admiring those works of art, the queen silently watched the gentle, modest girl. Turning at last to the king, she said: "I am satisfied; she is worthy the honor you have given her."

Long after this, while Hilma was one day gazing with love and happiness upon the precious babe in her arms, a lady silently entered the apartment and advanced toward her. She looked steadfastly upon the innocent babe, stooped and kissed it, gave her lovely hand to the mother, then left the room. It needed no one to tell Hilma the secret so like a blessing and love —it was the queen.

Thus envy did its work, but not as it intended. Affliction and sorrow were in that case blessings in disguise, and Hilma's goodness was her own reward, and became the pride and comfort of her humble parents. The story of her meeting the king endeared her to the people, and they also honored him and his noble queen for their course.

Their children attained to all that could be desired in the wishes of the countrymen, and they, loving them tenderly, bestowed titles and positions upon them.

Last Lines.

To children far, and children near,
Who'll read the things I've written here:
    From your young lives these things I took;
And many a mother I hear say,
"From out *my* darling's work and play
    I might write just as true a book."

Now when you close these simple leaves,
And happy thoughts your fancy weaves,
    Remember me, who sent you this;
And should we meet, or should we not,
I pray you all "forget me not,"
    And each accept a loving kiss.